DIARY OF A 'FLYGIRL' WANNABE:

(Life Lessons of a Cool Girl in Training)

BY
Carol Gee

Venuschronicles@aol.com

PublishAmerica

Baltimore

First printing

ISBN: 1-4137-1408-0
PUBLISHED BY PUBLISHAMERICA, LLLP
www.publishamerica.com
Baltimore

Printed in the United States of America

Dedication

This book is dedicated to women (and men) everywhere whose stories of struggle and search for self portray our shared humanity. It is dedicated to all whose life lessons are plentiful, where that mantra 'hardships breed character' becomes life's self-fulfilling prophecy of speaking 'truth to power' as we navigate our rites of passage.

To Janice
The journey
Continues
Carol

Acknowledgments

First I give thanks to my Creator for helping me to enrich the lives of others through words. Not too long ago it seems that I penned acknowledgments for my debut book, "The Venus Chronicles: Musings from the Feminine Side." Thanks to the love, support, and encouragement of both women and men, "Venus" continues to delight, inspire, and forge a sense of 'sisterhood' among women everywhere. While it seemed I probably thanked everyone under the sun back then, my list of gratitude continues to grow.

To Ronnie, my best friend and soul mate who has always supported my every endeavor, on whose shoulders I lean daily, thank you for loving me. To Barb and Michael, bonded by blood; to my 'sisters' at Emory University and the Centers for Disease Control and Prevention, (CDC), bonded by friendship, who clamor for this book and all the books that hopefully will follow; to Mardi, a hell of beautician and the 'girls' at the shop: Yo, Mary, Mary, (there are two Marys) and Pam; To members of my 'posse' Joyce, Marcia, Marymal, Kathleen, Valerie, Cynthia at FAMU (Florida A& M university); to Doc, Robert, Jim G. and Ron; to the two Carolyns, one in Oklahoma and the other one in Virginia, both long time friends of twenty to thirty years respectively; to my 'adopted' goddaughter, Yolanda, a lovely, young woman and gifted attorney; to my 'godsons' Gordon, Jason, Alfred, and Jameric.

Many thanks to Kelley and MaryAnn of Innerlight Publishing to whom I will be eternally grateful for giving me my literary publishing start.

I would like to thank the following authors for their support and encouragement. Their vision, creativity and imagination blow me away as they strive to raise the bar on literary excellence: To Valerie Boyd, whose masterpiece on the life of Zora Neale Hurston is beyond superb, and whose introduction to the publisher, and input to the project was one of the forces behind "The Venus Chronicles." To Zane, who books are hot, hot, hot. Don't extinguish the fire my sister. To Brother Maurice Gray, "To Whom Much is Given" and the sequel coming soon, your unselfishness knows no bounds. Thank you for your willingness to share lessons learned. To Kevin Johnson for your books promoting faith and spiritual health. To Tracy Price Thompson, a fellow sister-soldier whose debut book, "Black Coffee," showed the human side of those of us who *choose* to 'do more before noon than some folks do all day' to make the world a safer place: the military male and military female. Like me, Tracy has never met a stranger.

I want to thank the bookstores: African Spectrum, Chapter 11 Emory, MEDU, Nubian Books, and a big, big thanks to Charis Books and More in Atlanta who continue to keep "Venus" on their shelves and promote it, and to stores outside Georgia who are carrying it. I want to thank Rob and his staff at Emory Village Flowers and Gifts who helped to promote my book in their shop, and Anna's Wardrobe, (both of them located in Decatur Georgia), and other specialty shops who continue to express interest in carrying it. I want to thank the radio stations in Atlanta, that had me on the air, Twanda Black, KISS 104.1; Charone Pagett of 89.3FM and television station; "A Woman's Place." Angela, my host and I had a great time. A big thank you to Sharon Kay, host of "What's the 411?" WQQK, FM, (92Q) in Nashville for the opportunity to do a live call-in show, (that was great) to my other radio hosts, Gwen in New York and to LaRita Shelby, LA/ North Hollywood, 'Pookie' from "It's Your World" soap on The Tom Joyner Morning Show. I would like to thank Rolling Out, an urban newspaper in Atlanta for promoting it. I would like to thank Teresa at the Atlanta Journal and Constitution for posting my readings and public appearances. Finally I want to thank all the literary clubs, women's groups, and others who invited me to speak. My sincere appreciation goes out to everyone who bought "Venus," and to those of you who daily discover creative outlets to help me sell books. You are truly loved and appreciated.

I write about the black experience, but I am always talking about the human condition-about what we can endure, dream, fail at, and still survive.

Maya Angelou

FLYGIRL:
A female who 'really has it going on.' She is smart and self-confident. She's a sharp dresser, but with a style that's all her own. She seemingly knows all the right moves, does all the right things. She sets her own standards. People love her; hate her, try to emulate and imitate her.

Youth

Girlhood,
The journey of cornrows braided tight,
And pigtails
With skinny legs, sleek from Vaseline
Keeping time with the twirl of double Dutch ropes,
And the singsong rhythm of childhood rhymes

Where lipstick replacing bubble gum
Is only a hop, skip and jump away
From love, marriage and happily ever after
Strolling down the street behind a baby carriage

Too soon the sleek covers of Cosmo
Vies with Modern Maturity while
The words grandma and nana yelled at the top
Of small voices tugs on heartstrings now tender

Youth, sweet, sweet Dandelion puffs
Awaiting the breath of time
To blow softly upon it
Before disappearing into infinity

GROWN FOLKS' BUSINESS

Dear Diary:

Grown Folks' Business

"This is grown folks' business, you girls go sit down somewhere," mother used to tell us if we happened to be around where adults were gathered. Or if we questioned something that we heard and didn't understand. Never mind that we were already in the room before the adults came. So is it any wonder that when I became an adult I was ignorant of the ways of men and women? Or that I couldn't recognize the symptoms of PMS from a simple case of toe cramps. Or knew what happened when a woman went through 'the change'? According to my mother we had plenty of time to learn all that stuff.

Embracing the idea that children should be seen and not heard, we were batted away like flies from a room when adults were assembled. Naturally I blamed this banishment on my sister. For I was clever and kept as quiet as I could when grownups were talking, no mean feat. But my sister simply could not resist adding her two cents worth to any conversation.

Once as I sat quietly by playing hairdresser with my dolls, who by now all could have used Rogaine to combat further hair loss, trying to hear what I could hear, my sister ruined it. What the adults were talking about at the time I cannot recall. However, I remember that during a lull in the conversation, my sister, in the loudest voice known to mankind or at least it seemed like it at the time, asked our

17

guests if they wanted to see mother take her teeth out and put them back in? At seven she seemed unduly impressed by mother's dental work and really thought this was a neat trick. So, from then on, we were sent outside to ride our bikes, or to go watch television, or go clean our room; which parents know will get rid of you temporarily. Depending on how messy a child's bedroom is, parents might not see them for months.

By gleaning *some* stuff from their conversations, I knew that one of our neighbors had a common-law husband. I didn't know what that meant, except that it was said in such a hushed manner that I figured that it was something worth remembering. It wasn't until I was grown, that I learned that after seven years of living together without the benefit of clergy and ugly bridesmaid dresses that the law declared you legally married and in some states that entitled you to a property settlement in the event that you split up.

I learned that Sister Jones from our church was going through 'the change' and that her poor husband was catching pure HELL. Now that I could believe even if I didn't know what 'the change' was, as Sister Jones was well over six feet tall, while her husband was about five foot or perhaps a little taller. I wondered if those roots that Sister Jones supposedly was always working had somehow brought on this 'change'. I had no idea what roots were either. Yet I was frightened about the things that I heard they made people do.

I suspect that keeping us from learning about the harsh realities of life were parents' way of protecting their children and keeping them innocent as long as they could. Still, I often felt that shielding things from us kept us from learning necessary survival skills once we were out on our own.

Things like what to do about all those raging hormones, and the restorative powers of cold showers. By forbidding us to associate with some children, many of us didn't know how to get along with different people, or recognize those people who did not have our best interests at heart.

While I am not a parent, I *am* a mentor and a friend. So I invite the hard questions about life and love from my charges. Our conversations cover a lot of what was often deemed grown folks' business. And while I have been grown for a *long* time now, I find from our many conversations that I still have *a lot* to learn. And this keeps me young.

Dating

It has been a while since I have dated. I am sure that this comes as great news to my husband. Women friends say that dating is not what it used to be. Back when I *was* dating, I went to the movies, I went to dinner and the only thing I worried about was would he try to kiss me on the first date? And if I let him, would he think that I was easy? Would he expect that tongue thing? Alas, my mother's rules of dating etiquette have gone by the wayside.

It seems like there are so many things to worry about besides checking our handbags for breath mints before indulging in that kiss with or without tongue. Today women must know their date's health history. They ponder if they should ask to see a current health record, truly a new twist on the old 'you show me yours, and I'll show you mine'; along with a firm directive that every date must wear a rain coat (a condom), even when there is only a slim chance of rain in the dating forecast.

They worry that when they return from freshening up in the powder room, they will find that their beverage of choice has been doctored, so that waking up the next morning holding onto their head to keep it from falling off is now a *good* thing. Women should insist on a fresh beverage without feeling guilty about waste.

Yes Virginia, while there may or may not be a Santa Claus the dating rules they are a-changing. A co-worker told me that where she was from if you allow a man to buy you a beer and get him to slide down the bar peanuts that's considered a first date. While in other areas that she had heard of they believe that brushing knees with a member of the opposite sex signified a second date. Who knew? She said that she is exploring other parts of the country to research their dating rituals and is checking to see if Air Tran flies there. She promised to publish her report on her web site, www.datenuts.com

Alas, men and women both have dating horror stories, although women are more prone to share them. Two such stories immediately come to mind. For example, not long ago my god-daughter was visiting and, like most of our communications, the subject of dating comes up, as she, like a lot of women, is seeking someone nice who might be interested in commitment and maybe marriage.

Her most recent date at that time had been a date with a guy who had invited her to a car and boat auction. She said that after viewing what seemed like a million cars and a few boats in a three-hour time period, he asked her if she was hungry. Like me, she can't remember a time ever that she was not hungry, except perhaps in her sleep.

She said it was around 1:30 on a mild Saturday so, after much discussion about their options, they decided on Captain D's which was nearby as her date had seen a car or two that he thought he might bid on when the bidding began in another hour. When they got in the restaurant, however, he asked her is she minded if they could split a fish platter. My friend, already tired and bored, was now angry. She thought that had they been in really nice restaurant and he had suggested this, it might not have been so bad. Why it might have seemed kind of intimate. But his asking to split fake fish she felt was the height of insults. After all, this was a professional man who planned to bid and perhaps purchase a car for goodness sakes.

Another of my 'adopted' god-children, a young man who until recently could have co-starred in that Burt Reynolds movie, "The Man who Loved Women" made me laugh when he shared with me that some time ago, after a particular date, the lady in question, on her way out the door of his apartment, told him that after that date that she had decided to embrace Celibacy. Her church had been hosting classes on abstinence whereupon graduating the women wore white gowns and rings symbolizing this new commitment. She said that she had been contemplating it for a time, but he had helped her to make up her mind.

Then there was the episode that I called the 'Hot Wing' drama, where, during a date with this same young man, a volatile young woman, fed up with all his game-playing, threw a pan of hot wings in his face. As he described how he felt as hot wing sauce dripped down his face, all I could think about was *man, what a waste of good wings*, and wished that I had some.

Growing up in the same neighborhood practically my whole life was not conducive to meeting boys. For daily I came face to face with the same boys who knew me when I was skinny and had nothing to put in a bra. The few brave souls who ventured into our neighborhood to see me were interrogated by the 'date police' (my mother) with questions like, "You don't live in the neighborhood do you?" "Do I know your people?" she would ask, giving my hapless date the once-over. A look that said she knew his intentions to her baby and did not like them.

Few survived the inquisition, which was fine for mother who felt that even at almost twenty years old I was too young to date. Once a patron of her beauty shop asked her if I was dating, to which my mother replied, "No she's not. She is only nineteen years old. She has plenty of time to do that. Right now she is trying to decide what

CAROL GEE

she wants to do with her life."

What I decided to do with my life was join the Air Force. Here I played simulated war games alongside a few of my male counterparts. With others I played the dating game. Too soon I discovered that many of my dates thought that the Air Force's slogan, "Aim high," meant my breasts. And while many appeared to be normal guys, in a darkened movie theater I wondered where they hid all their hands during the day.

So it was quite refreshing that the guy who would become my husband was a gentleman on our dates. Our first date ended with a kiss on my forehead, as did the second. By the third, however, I wanted to scream, what's with the forehead, I have lips? Years later he confessed that his strategy to win me over was to be different from all my other dates. His strategy worked.

After many years of marriage he and I still go on dates once or twice or month. It may be as simple as a trip to Wal-Mart, or to the movies, or as elaborate as a dinner in one of Atlanta's finest restaurants. The place less important than the time spent in each other's company, laughing, talking and reconnecting.

So I say to all those women out there dating or trying to make a love connection something my mother used to tell me. She said if a woman does not stand for something, sadly she will fall for anything. And that has made all the difference in my life.

24

PMS

On my road to life I have just about given up reading the newspaper and relegated myself to reading bumper stickers instead. You know, "Honk if you hate my driving," "Call 1-800-Road Rage," or "My child is an honor student at Smart Kids Elementary." The ones I truly like are: "I brake for yard sales" and "BINGO *is too* my middle name." Like a tailgater, those are the ones I follow. However one day I found myself stopped behind a blue Honda whose bumper sticker truly summed it up for me. It read: "I have PMS and I've got a gun."

For women, (PMS) Premenstrual Syndrome is often the bane of their existence. It's right up there with that one gray hair that keeps coming back in your otherwise perfectly arched dark eyebrow. And it's different from one woman to another. When you are young, you might feel a little cranky and bloated for several days, which my mother chalked up to a just a phase that I was going through and that I had better get over it soon, if I knew like she knew.

As we age new symptoms crop up almost overnight. There are the lightening fits of anger that quickly evaporates into tears. You find yourself crying at cereal commercials. "Why, oh why won't those horrible kids let that poor rabbit have any TRIXs?" You cry for days in a row sending family and friends scurrying for cover when you enter a room. You cry at that. You keep tissues handy, tucked inside the cleavage of your bosom. They don't fall out. You cry at that.

Hormones cloud your vision and the word *divorce* comes to mind more often that not. Particularly when your spouse does something you consider strange, like leaving every drawer or door open everywhere drawers and doors exist. Where leaning on the refrigerator door eyeing its content has become his new spectator sport. Or a trail of breadcrumbs can be traced back to where he recently made a sandwich. Okay I admit it. It took me a while to realize that, unlike milk, my husband simply didn't just 'go bad' once a month.

Oh to have PMS, without a Snickers bar in sight. You feel like baying at the moon. You find yourself screaming when a whisper would do. You are bloated and your head and back are killing you. You get this craving for salt and chocolate that will not go away until you have devoured a Snickers and Lays Potato Chip sandwich.

What happened to the easygoing person that people used to think you were? Suddenly this gentle soul, this easygoing woman has turned into hurricane Carol, Linda or Joyce where even your pets scramble to hide for they know that as much as you adore them and would not hurt them for the world, that when this happens, not even they are safe.

Only recently recognized as a problem, Hippocrates (often called the Father of Modern Medicine) wrote about these symptoms a thousand years ago. The World Health Organization has stated in a report that only one premenstrual symptom is actually needed to diagnose PMS. Throw in lack of appetite, soreness, and other complaints and you know it's not all in your mind as some have thought.

Fortunately, PMS does not last forever. Although the only known cure is menopause, or the 'change' as it's often called, which of course comes with its own issues. Still I was having lunch recently with a friend who is also a physician when I mentioned my occasional bouts with PMS, and she offered me the perfect solution. It was so simple I don't know why I didn't think of it. Looking me in the eye, she said, "Go home take two Butterfingers and call me in the morning."

Isn't it Romantic?

Ask anyone who is more romantic, men or women, and many will say that women are, while others will say that men are. Many say that romance is in a woman's nature, and that they care more about that aspect in a relationship than men do. Even studies have suggested that women may be genetically and socially conditioned to be more romantic then men.

Scores of movies today cater to women's love of romance. Buy a box of Kleenex and go to any so-called chick movie and watch as women cry and sigh throughout the show. Their dates also sigh. They fidget in their seats and keep checking their watches wishing that they were anyplace else but there. While women like movies offering mystery and romance, men tend to love heavy testosterone films with action and fighting throughout the entire flick. Any romance in these films may be the occasional romp in the sack between the lead male and his half-naked co-star.

While women appear to be better with words, boys are often taught that revealing emotions may be construed as a sign of weakness, as does any displays of tenderness. Growing up, we girls played Wedding Barbie with Ken as the spouse, while little boys played with GI Joe and matchbox cars. While no one knows whatever happened to Ken, it has been rumored that he and GI Joe are now an item, and have taken up housekeeping at Barbie's house in Malibu. However Barbie is still around and still dressing in those sexy outfits in order to attract men. Other action figures have long replaced GI Joe but the focus is still on action and heroics.

So, what does being romantic mean? Is it only about candlelight and roses? When I was first married, while I harbored secret thoughts of lace camisoles and sexy black nighties, my husband bought me household items. One Christmas, he gave me a four-slice toaster. When I reminded him that we had received three toasters as wedding gifts (how much toast did people think I ate) and that I had given two of them away, he indicated that this one was better as I could toast four slices instead of two. Poor thing, he thought that he was making things easier for me. How could that be wrong?

On my birthday that year he bought me a mixer, a Sunbeam, which was top of the line in appliances back then. Still I didn't say anything until my kitchen appliances were completed. Because you know what they say: blenders are like men, you always feel that you need one, you just don't know why.

Men have been known to use romance to win the hearts of women when they want to, demonstrating that they can be romantic when need be. But in my opinion, romance is more about action then words. Although I am told that men imploring women to "Come on girl, get up off of that thang" still works for some women.

Still,I have always been a romantic. Maybe its because I was born three days before Valentine's Day. I spend a lot of time planning romance in my life. Case in point. A couple of weeks ago, after an extremely difficult workweek, I thought I would take a long soak in a tub full of bubbles, thinking that would relax me.

I poured in some strawberry bubble bath, followed with some strawberry bath salts. I tuned the Shower Tunes radio hanging on the bathroom wall to "Jazz Flavors." While the tub filled, I lit some candles around the room as well as a stick of incense that put me in mind of some place far away. I thought that I would invite my husband to join me as he too had had a rough week. And by now his hand must be tired from all that clicking of the remote controls as he surfed the channels on the two televisions that he has in the upstairs sitting room. I pictured us cuddling in the warm, delicious-smelling water, maybe scrubbing each other's back, a rare treat.

The bubbles now nearing the top of the deep bathtub I bent to cut the water off. Running my hand under the flowing water one last time, I got the shock of my life. Somehow while I fantasized about Calgon and my husband's arms taking me away, my hot water had turned cold. Calling out for him to go downstairs and check the water heater, I ran my hands through my tub full of bubbles to find them lukewarm at best.

My husband returned upstairs stating that nothing appeared to be wrong with the water heater. However this was my fantasy, I was not to be denied. Handing him a bath sponge I asked him to scrub my back. Of course now he did so standing outside the bathtub instead of in. And he was fully clothed. But it still felt great. To this day we never knew what happened to the water heater; some sort of power surge I suspect, as the next morning it was fine and has been fine ever since.

Being romantic is about intimacy. It's being generous with feelings and emotions. Not long ago I asked my husband what he thought has kept us together all these years. He replied that he never knew what I was going to do from one minute to the next and that he found that exciting. He also said that I had this uncanny ability to make him laugh.

I was hoping that he would say it was because he still found my body to be 'bootylicious' or something like that. Oh well. Still, whether it's laughing together over some shared joke, eating a salad from a fast-food restaurant off your good china in your dining room, or his holding your hand while you are crossing the street that makes you feel loved and cherished, being romantic simply means creating those special moments that touch each other's souls.

Good Girls

Okay, I admit it. When I was growing up I wanted to be bad. I don't mean the kind of *bad* where I was arrested and forced to wear an orange jumpsuit. I wanted to be the kind of bad where big earrings dangled from my pierced ears and tight jeans called attention to my budding shape. A long ponytail would swing from side to side when I walked. I wanted to be the girl that all the 'fly' girls looked up to and all the 'fly' boys wanted to date. I wanted a leather coat. My mother, however, would not hear of it. I was going to be a good girl, and that was all there was to it. Her idea of "Girls Gone Wild" was failure to wash dishes or not combing my 'kitchen' (the hair at back of your head, right above your neck).

My Sunday school and stayed-all-day-in-church family was set on raising good girls. Good girls as I understood the concept, did not wear clothes that caused unwanted attention to themselves. Nor did they wear red shoes or anything else in that color. And they did not wear white shoes after Labor Day. They did not call boys, or have out-of-wedlock anything. If they did, they did not live under my mothers "roof and eat her meat and bread," thank you very much.

I remember it still. I was about fourteen years old. We were visiting my favorite aunt in Virginia, something we did every summer in August. As my mother and aunt sat on the front porch, a neighbor walked by, saw them, and stopped to chat. I came out to ask my mother a question wearing some old shorts that had grown a little snug on my budding figure. As I turned to go back into the house, I heard the man say "your daughter is cute, looks like she is about ready to cut the mustard." Now, I was not sure what that meant (I thought it was probably one of those country expressions, not heard of in Washington, DC where we lived). But my mother must have known what it meant, because she responded in that voice that often stopped people in their tracks, "I had better not catch her doing it." The visitor soon left.

Good girl lessons began early in a girl's life. Good girls did not chew gum. And they certainly did not crack it. Good girls didn't cross their legs except at the ankles. Good girls sat a certain way, and acted a certain way. For as long as I can remember my mother told me that boys can wallow in the mud and get up and still be considered a boy, but a girl wallowing in the mud, well she just got muddy.

'Sugar and Spice and every thing nice'. That's what little girls are made of. 'Nice' meaning easy-going, never making waves. Even in fairy tales, girls were 'nice'. Take Cinderella for instance. She was always cheerful even in the wake of cruelty and abuse at the hands of her wicked stepmother and ugly sisters. She should have just jet-slapped them a couple of times and they would have left her alone.

Snow White was another one. Just like a good girl believing that an apple a day kept the evil away. Had she liked, say, tangerines or could have afforded oranges perhaps the wicked witch might have not have tried to poison her. Still these fables present two sides of womanhood: the 'good' girl, pretty, smiling, nice, and the despised one, evil, always jealous, always angry.

Good girls often found themselves trying to live up other people's perception, only to end up feeling depressed and anxious when they feel that they have let people down. Because good girls do not get angry. We've all heard this nursery rhyme:

There was a little girl who had a little curl
Right in the middle of her forehead.
And, when she was good, she was very, very good.
But when she was bad, she was horrid.

As adults many of us continue to carry these lessons on being nice around with us. We walk around on eggshells in relationships so as not to offend others or hurt their feelings, even at the risk of our own feelings and emotions. Even in our intimate relationships the 'good girl' spills over. "You want me to do what?" we ask. Or "I don't think the chandelier people had that in mind when they designed it." Good Girls avoid confrontation at all cost. How many times have you thought of things that you should have said long after a confrontation was over, and kicked yourself for not taking a stand and saying them? Anger that is suppressed often comes out in inappropriate ways and times.

At some point we must stop worrying about others' expectations of us and simply be ourselves. So with our newly found freedom we cross our legs over our knees. With glee we loudly crack a stick of gum, happy to know that, with our crowns and bridge work, we can. Neither a good girl, nor a bad one, simply females allowing themselves to have some fun.

Satin Sheets

Once upon a time only royalty could afford the sensual elegance of silk and satin sheets. So my being a princess, at least in my own mind, I longed for some. In my mind's eye I saw myself reclining in a 'glamour shot' pose on red or black satin sheets. In this picture I would be wearing a beautiful peignoir like those women on Dynasty and Melrose Place. Lying next to me would be my spouse gazing lovingly into my eyes. In *my* fantasy, there would be no potato chip or cracker crumbs from eating snacks in bed, or cat hair, like in real life.

This fantasy came true when my husband and I returned to the states after having spent three years in Okinawa with the Air Force. We accepted an invitation to spend a few days with friends in San Francisco before heading to our new duty station. Like most, our hosts gave up their bedroom where the lady made up the bed with a brand new set of red satin sheets straight out of the package. How had she known about my fantasy?

Giddy with anticipation I jumped into the shower with my thoughts on what lie ahead. I imagined holding each other close bathed in the afterglow of lovemaking so good that afterwards the neighbors on both sides of the condo had a cigarette. Unfortunately this is where fantasy and reality collided–big time. It started with his pillow sliding to the floor with a skidding sound. My pillow followed next.

You've heard of Kung fu fighting? This was more like Kungfu lovemaking. Ouch! The sheets felt like ice against my warm flesh. POW! There went my elbow to his ribs when I reached out to hug him. My so-called sensual kiss missed his mouth altogether and we ended rubbing noses. I have heard that this is the way that Eskimos do it, and, hey, to each his own. But this was not part of my fantasy.

During one point in our 'love dance,' I must have made a move that my spouse interpreted as sexy, for I watched the hazel in his eyes change like it does at *those* times. In reality, I was trying for a position that I hoped would keep me from flying across the bed. For I don't care what others think, falling out the bed on my head is not considered foreplay, at least not to me.

Then my leg cramped up. He had to help me rub it out. Needless to say, we got no sleep that night or anything else. I laid in one spot most of the night, fearful that I might fall out of bed at any given time if I moved. We both woke up looking like something one of our kitties had dragged in. Thank goodness, I had not bought those sheets as I suspect they would have ended as the prettiest satin curtains that people had ever seen in my guest bathroom.

Over the years I have discovered that each stage of life brings with it its own set of expectations. The texture of love is no exception. Sometimes it's satiny smooth; full and rich like the deepest chocolate. Other times, love is as rough and rocky as the tide. I still recall the bedroom gymnastics of our youth, and from time-to-time we revisit them, if for nothing else to prove to ourselves that we can, after three decades of marriage. Still, the best kind of relationship for most is soft and tender, the kind one gets from someone familiar and dear. Much like cotton or flannel, it's natural and durable.

As we indulge ourselves with fantasies, we are reminded that everything that looks good, often times is not. At long last we take comfort in the knowledge that it is okay to be cotton percale, or even flannel, in a satin sheet world.

The Way Men and Women Communicate

Men and women share different perspectives on most things. Communication is no exception. Remember the first time you decided to travel to someplace outside the US? Most likely the first thing you did right after getting a passport was ran out and bought an English/ Foreign Language Dictionary. The languages abound, English/Spanish, English/French, English/ German, English/English, like in the country of England, where a *fag* is a cigarette and not someone calling you a name. You practiced saying common phrases for each country. Good Morning. How are you? Where is the restroom? How much are those shoes? You learned the names for all the important food groups: eggs, bread, Scotch. Your bags were packed and you were ready to go.

But the first time you spoke your first foreign word, your host looked at you like you had two heads. So you tried another word, this time pointing and using arm gestures. They burst out laughing. He is probably thinking, crazy Americans; they sure pick strange moments to dance. Then you start to panic. You think, man, what is that word again for Scotch?

Communicating with a man is a lot like that. We have all been there: You are trying to have a discussion with a man. You are talking your heart out, explaining, gesturing with your hand for emphasis.

41

CAROL GEE

While he is simply sitting there on the couch, on the bed, wherever, not saying a thing. You stop mid-sentence, your hands on your hips and ask in a loud voice, "Are you listening to me?" He snaps out of his fantasy of buying that golf club with the money he won on the football pool. Quickly he responds that he is listening. The next thing out of your mouth that he knows is coming, you ask, "What I was talking about? What was I saying?"

You simply want him to acknowledge that he is listening, by saying something, asking a question, say hmm, or uh-huh, something. The way our girlfriends do. Men don't do that. After all, many have realized early on in the relationship that a closed mouth gathers no foot. They wouldn't even think of interrupting. Like our girlfriends do. Which, truth to tell, can actually get on our nerves when we have a juicy story to tell and they keep interrupting.

We get impatient with our partner when he is trying to express himself. You wish that he would get on with what he is trying to say. We put words in his mouth. He says, "I got a raise on my job. I think we should...." And before he can say another thing, we have filled in the blanks: go on a cruise, buy a new car, and go to Cancun. He is thinking: invest, or maybe paint the house.

And we are too vague when we talk with men. We say,"We need to talk." (He is thinking, oh heck, what now?)
"What about?" he says.
"We need to talk about our relationship." we say.
"What's wrong with our relationships?" he asks.
Sound familiar? Instead of being vague we need to ask for what we want. Then there can be no mistakes, no guessing that he or she understands what we are talking about, and no misunderstandings.

Men say that women always want to communicate. And we set them up with four little words that men hate. No, it isn't "not tonight, I've got a headache." That's six words, although men hate them too.

42

I am talking about those *other* four little words: *"What are you thinking?"* Men *hate* this. For where it seems to us that most of the time men are not thinking. From some of the things that they sometimes do, I have found that men are often deep thinkers. They are just not used to thinking about *feelings*, or talking about emotions. Most men are not comfortable putting their thoughts into words and hate to be put on the spot. Of course then we think that they are not sensitive. I have learned to stop pressuring my man to talk. For I have discovered it does not work.

I have learned that when a man is ready to share with you, he will, on his own, in his own time, *if we create the space* where he is comfortable sharing. For me this usually happens when we are riding in the car together, perhaps running some errands or headed for some destination. Simple questions like, "what's going on at work?" in a casual manner can get him to open up.

Followed on the heels of what are you thinking is, "Do you love me?" "Does this dress make me look fat?" Or, "Do you think that she is prettier than I am?" when we spot him glancing at another female. Finally there is my personal favorite, and I admit I have asked it. "What would you do if I died?"

Which right about now your man is probably thinking, "Is that likely to happen anytime soon, like before I have to answer these questions?" For he knows that the answer to any of these questions will probably not get him anywhere near to *pillow talk* tonight or anytime soon.

Often, the communication process is much like a dance where both partners are trying to lead. The steps can be subtle like in body language or you can bang smack into each other with words. Some of us will recognize ourselves here:

The loud sigh–did you hear it? It says it all doesn't it? It means what an idiot. Was he like this when we were dating?

The word *fine*, used at the end of every argument. From the tone of it, you know that things are definitely not fine. And men have learned not to use it to answer the trick question: "How do I look?"

Go ahead...really means, you can go ahead if you want buddy, but you will have HELL to pay later.

Thanks a lot. This is *not* an expression of gratitude. It means thanks for not supporting me or backing me up. This is usually followed by a loud sigh; sometimes referred to as the double whammy for while an actual word wasn't uttered, the message is still loud and clear. Remember doing this as a child after your mother had scolded you for something, and she looked you in the eye and asked if you had something to say?

Whatever, this is usually followed by a hand held up in front of your face like a stop sign. It's like saying; "you are dismissed." More than likely this will not be the *end* to your conversation.

Ok I admit it, after thirty years of marriage I am still guilty of these so-called weird conversations with my spouse. In truth, I only ask him if he still loves me or what he would do if I died every now and then, just to take the edge off. And it truly is coincidental that these urges take place when he is trying to watch the championship playoff of Badminton or some other sport and not some fiendish plot to drive him insane. Honest. Still if he would cut down the sound, stop that incessant hand movement that seems to occur whenever he puts down the remote listen to me for a few minutes, and murmur in all the right places, I swear they would not take long.

Still, despite all those books on communicating, women know that, no matter what, a typical communication will begin with: "Honey, while you are up, can you get me a cup of coffee, a beer, a glass of water?" (fill in the blanks), and end with "You paid *HOW MUCH* for that?" And while it appears that men often speak in a language that is totally foreign to women, they are well...communicating. And frankly that's a start.

Real Life Vs Fairy Tales

I was seven years old when I got my first library card. What a wonderful day that was. I chose books like other children chose candy, and I couldn't wait to get them home so I could escape between the pages. Sometimes my mother had to call me several times to come to dinner.

The Bobbsey Twins, which was one of the longest-running series of books back then, was one of my favorite books. There were two sets of twins: Bert and Nan, who were the oldest, with dark hair and dark eyes, and Freddie and Flossie, fair of hair with blue eyes. They lived on Lake Metoka in somewhere, USA with two black servants; a cook named Dinah and Sam who, I suspect, did everything else. How different they were from me, an inner-city child with brown skin and long braids and working-class parents. Still, as a child I was carried away on their adventures to the country to visit Uncle Daniel, often taking the family dog Snap and the family cat Snoop along for the ride. Their life was really a fairy tale, for no one I knew lived like that.

There were the fairy tales, Snow White and the Seven Dwarfs, Little Red Riding Hood, and Henny Penny. According to the story, Snow White lived in the woods with seven Dwarfs, who left for work every day whistling "Hi Ho, Hi Ho, it's off to work we go," while Snow stayed home and, I guess, kept house. Now that I think about it, where the heck did they work that they were so happy that they sang about it? And what was really going on back there in the woods? Why was Grumpy so grumpy? And was Doc really a doctor? If he was, why didn't he give Sneezie something to stop him from sneezing?

And what was with little Red Riding Hood? Didn't her mother ever warn her about the big, bad wolf? Although I have to hand it to her, that red cape was nice. Unfortunately today many children grow up knowing about the big, bad wolf. As little as three years old, children are warned never to talk to strangers; that some touches are good while others are bad. Sadder still is that to some boys and girls the 'bad, wolf' is sometimes dad, or grandpa, or a family friend.

Much like Chicken Little, you can always find someone who is the voice of doom crying "Oh me, oh my, the sky is falling, my dog has fleas, this acid rain is ruining my weave." These are people who see the negative side of everything. And many of us have learned that, like in the fairytales, if you want some thing done right, you have to do it yourself. If you don't believe it, ask any woman with a husband or kids.

In some relationships, a few still find it hard to separate reality from fairy tales, white lies from the truth. Though few women today still believe that their prince is going to come charging in on a white horse, wake them with a kiss, and take them away from it all. If he does come, we think, he had better come bearing a giant pooper-scooper, because we are *not* cleaning that up.

Real life is not a fairy tale. But it is possible to experience sunshine even on cloudy days with the right person by your side. Still ,it's important for us to remember a couple of things. In real life, 'you *can* love the one you are with.' And 'rainy days and Mondays' don't *always* have to get you down.

Loving You

Recently, as part of my annual physical, my doctor recommended that I get a colonoscopy, a procedure that exams your colon for cancerous conditions. In a matter-of-fact voice, he explained that during the exam they would run a lighted scope through my rectum and up into my colon. Without thinking, I grabbed my backside in protection. My doctor, seeing my reaction, burst out laughing.

From the time that we are born, we are poked, prodded and stuck with needles, all in the name of good health. There are childhood immunizations, school vaccinations, and immunizations needed to travel to parts far and wide. So the tests and examinations that come with middle age shouldn't have surprised me. With a referral slip in hand and much trepidation, I made an appointment with a specialist who would perform the exam.

The pamphlet that he gave me informed me about all the things that could go wrong. They ranged from possible bleeding from the rectum, (yuck) to cramps, to cardiac arrest. How far *up* are they planning to go I thought? However, with no known family history of colon cancer, knock on wood, and never having experienced any colon problems to my knowledge, the doctor recommended the modified procedure which did not require me to be put to sleep, which still failed to calm me.

CAROL GEE

The night before the exam that was scheduled took place, I performed step one of a two-step process. First I had to drink a small bottle of a citrus-like liquid that cleanses the colon. (Translation, prepare to spend *the night* in the restroom) Though it wasn't until I attempted step two, the dreaded enema to clean out anything that could possibly be left in my colon after step one, did the comedy began.

Realizing long ago from dance classes that not all people of color had rhythm this became my reality when I tried to adapt the pose on the back of the enema box. A diagram showed two ways to get comfortable. So, debating whether to lie on the bed or floor, I finally decided the floor was probably best. A decision that I soon discovered was the wisest one, when a few minutes later, I felt the liquid not going inside me like it was supposed to but running down my leg.

To further my humiliation, I looked up to see both of my cats sitting there staring at me. One decided to lie down on my foot–the one that weighs 18 pounds. I guess he didn't want to miss anything. While I swear the little tiger-colored one was smirking. Even I know that I must have looked a sight, flopping around on the carpet, butt up in the air, much like a beached whale in a pink nightdress. I could almost hear the oldest one speaking in that secret language of felines, "I am not sure what she is doing, but if she starts sniffing my butt I am *so* out of here." (Anyone who has ever had cats knows that this is how they recognize each other's scent).

I'm happy to say the procedure went smoothly. No sooner was I lying on my side covered with a warm hospital blanket, than a scope was threaded up into my colon. With just slightest hint of cramping, enough to make me take a deep breath, it was on its way out, all the while the doctor praising me for doing so well.

Feeling empowered that I had gone through with the procedure

50

gave me a great sense of accomplishment. For I had seriously considered calling and canceling my appointment. I even called the appointment desk to do just that. However, after talking to the male nurse who answered my questions, I decided to go ahead.

Many factors keep women (and men) from getting the exams and procedures that are required for us to maintain optimum health. Fear of the procedure, that it might hurt, and what the doctor might find (the old what I don't know, won't hurt me). But not knowing can hurt you.

Sure, several schools of thought abound concerning annual pap smears and mammograms. Still these go a long way in ruling out some health issues. Although I think that if the medical profession really wanted women to keep their Pap Smear appointments, they might wish to consider decorating. How about putting some leopard fur or tiger fur on those stirrups? Or painting a mural on the ceiling so that we would have something pretty to look at and keep our minds off the procedure. It would certainly cut down on that incessant humming that many of us do. Or is that just me? And how about warming those instruments before poking us with them?

In all seriousness though, in order to love someone else, we must first learn to love ourselves. Regular physical exams, and other procedures as well as regular visits to your dentist are certainly ways to start.

I Won't Dance, So Don't Ask Me

Music was always a part of my life when I was growing up. The radio would be on in the background in our house and you'd often hear my mother humming along to some tune. I played the violin in junior high, and I sang alto in both the glee club and our church choir.

However my mother didn't condone dancing. Instead of going around 'shaking myself,' she thought my time was better spent doing something constructive like chores around the house or studying Algebra. So, needless to say, I never quite mastered a lot of the popular dance steps. She did however like the old dances, the Waltz, the Virginia Reel, and all things that reminded her of her native Virginia. These dances she thought were quite graceful and wouldn't throw my back out like that Twist dance.

In the fifth grade we studied ballroom dancing. It was here that I discovered that I had no rhythm. Two left feet attempting a curtsy (bowing from the waist with my feet crossed simultaneously) is hard on a person's balance I determined while dancing the Waltz. So the dance The Twist was a natural for me. Why, I was the Twist Princess! Behind closed doors I practiced going down low to the floor and back up much like a spinning top. Sometimes I twisted with my left leg up, other times with the right. In secret, Chubby Checker and I twisted the night away.

The Electric Slide and those other line dances seem so easy when others are doing it. But when I attempt them, I am about as graceful as a buffalo wearing high heels. When others are sliding to the right, somehow I am always sliding left. So at clubs I sat like a wallflower while all around me people are 'getting jiggy' with it.

Like many women, my dance through life has often been uncoordinated and fraught with missteps on the road to maturity. It is my story, but I suspect that it's the story of growing up female in America. It's the story of trying hard to find one's niche.

The first thing that I did when I left home was pierce my ears, something my mother would not allow. I slept in on Sundays instead of going to church. I changed my hair, dying it a different color on a weekly basis. One week I was a redhead, the next a blonde. I was dying to find out if they really had more fun. Once it was even a weird shade of green. However that was a mistake and what you get with too dye and not enough coloring experience. Who knew that a young woman with green hair today would hardly rate a second glance?

I joined the Air Force to see the world and like my sisters in blue, I protested whatever war was raging at the time, whatever cause: "Save the whales, save the seals, save the rain forest." I shouted "Power to the People" and "I am Black and I am Proud" with my fists clinched and an arm adorned by a black armband when I was out of my blue uniform. But I questioned what it was all about when a fellow protestor tried to get me to lie down with him for the 'cause,' immediately calling me an Oreo when I refused. Call me crazy, but I don't 'dirty dance' with just anyone.

Still, I have heard it said that with age, comes wisdom. So after years of self-medicating with M&Ms, and crying through enough Kleenex to last a lifetime, I've gotten in touch with myself. The self that had absorbed childhood slights into my pores like steam, the feelings of never measuring up to my mother's or other people's expectations.

Finally I've quit crying because people have dismissed me for not being Black enough (culturally); not pretty enough; for not being *something*, enough. At last I have stopped dancing to other people's beat, and have begun dancing to the rhythm in my own soul. And guess what? I haven't missed a step since.

Mother's Day
(Better Known as the Baby Blues)

I love holidays. At Christmas, I deck my halls–not with balls of holly; that stuff hurts. But I drape tinsel and garland on everything that stands still. Even the cats know to stay away when I get that gleam in my eye. My tree, an artificial Scotch Pine, the one that I bought the first year that my husband and I were married, gets its pine scent courtesy of an air freshener disguised as an ornament tucked in its branches. Ornaments from our travels around the world with Uncle Sam co-exist with those brought from the 99-cent store. For I don't have to be an elf to enjoy this time of year. Thanksgiving I go all out with a turkey or ham and side dishes galore. And even though my cul-de-sac has few trick-or-treaters, I still buy a bag of candy at Halloween, and wait for some little ghost or goblin to ring my doorbell.

Mother's Day is a different story. For it has often been a day filled with emotions. As, unlike most women, my 'babies' don't have a head full of curly hair, or my husband's hazel eyes, but have four legs, a tail, and breath reeking of tuna. You see my husband and I make up a segment in society known as 'married without children.'

President Woodrow Wilson around 1914 declared the second

CAROL GEE

Sunday in May to be Mother's Day, as a way to reward women who spent 72 hours expelling a little person, often the size of a basketball, from their tummies. On this day moms are lavished with cards made in school bearing messages in fat, cursive letters that beat hands-down any sentiment mass-produced by Hallmark. Gifts, brunches and other activities round out her day.

Couples remain childless for many reasons. Infertility or other illness is usually the culprit. Like other couples, we suffered all the fertility tests. We made love on demand at different times of the day and night. That part was okay. I kept charts and stood on my head afterwards until I got dizzy and caught a cramp, to no avail. With no visible medical reasons our childless state forever remained a mystery to the doctors and to us.

Yet couples without children are often looked upon with pity, or made to feel badly for their childless state. We are subjected to personal questions. "How come you don't have children?" some will ask. "You'd make a great mother." How would *you* know, I think? Is there a sign on me that declares 'great mommy material' that I am unaware of?

These comments are usually followed by dire consequences. "You had better have children before you get too old," others say. Or "You should have some children, so that you will have somebody to take care of you when you get old." Call me crazy, but I don't think that one should have children so that they can be indebted to you for life, like I am with MasterCard. And how many people have you read about who have children, and still die alone in nursing homes because their children are too busy to care for them, or to even visit?

And yes, those of us who don't have children already know that we are probably missing out on a lot. The first steps, the first word and the joys of potty training. In my old age I am sure that someone will say that the reason for my all my illnesses, real or imagined, is

58

because I never rejoiced in near-lunatic abandon when my child went poop in the potty for the very first time. Nor have I really lived until my toddler has taken off her Pull-ups all by herself and announced it at the top of her little lungs to strangers in Wal-Mart as I blush like a fool.

Go ahead, label me 'mommy dearest' because I am not dying to hold every baby I see, or go around sniffing up its little baby essence. I love talcum powder and baby lotion as much as anyone. But those things I can *still* afford on my salary, unlike say, meat or oranges.

How would you know about the little *ache* childless women experience whenever we get around babies and small children, despite all of our bravado? Or the many times we have pretended that some cute little boy or girl was our own when we were babysitting or when we take them on an outing alone? For if you did, perhaps you might be a little less insensitive about insisting that we hold your baby. Or make fun of the way we hold them or act around them.

Being a mother is more than the incident of giving birth, it is one of life's great blessings. In an ideal world, every woman who longs for a child should be able to conceive them. But we all know that life is not fair. Because if it were, there would not be children born into families where they are abused, abandoned, even killed. In an ideal world every child would have a mother and a father.

Still, having spent much of my life as an educator and mentor I have always been surrounded by children, youth or young adults. Like all the cats that have owned me over the years, I have also been adopted by humans. So through the years I have discovered other ways that I could contribute to the lives of others. On Mother's Day I, too, receive telephone calls, cards, and gifts.

Just this past Mother's Day a card arrived in the mail, addressed to me from one of my 'adopted goddaughters.' While she has a mother, she has chosen me as her 'mother-figure.' On the front in big letters, it said *'Happy Mother's Day to My Mother.'* As tears rolled down my face, I counted my blessings. And I try to focus on all that I do have, instead of what I don't.

Resolutions

A few years ago I stopped making New Year's resolutions. I simply quit, just like that, cold turkey. After all, most of my resolutions didn't even last a week. The one where I was going to lose 30 pounds in 30 days only lasted a day, when I was confronted with a slice of homemade pound cake.

For how often do people actually bake *anything* from scratch today, with all of the 'just add water and it's on the table in twenty minutes' meals available? However, I tend to shy away from those products for they remind me too much of the 'ready to eat' meals, a staple for soldiers in the field that I was forced to live on more times than I care to remember.

Other resolutions lasted a little longer. The 'I will not nag my spouse about leaving every cabinet door open that he has opened in his search for a glass or a plate, even though they have been in the exact same place the entire ten years that we have lived in this house.' This one lasted until I bumped my head on one of the open cabinets. However the one where I resolved to treat others the way that I would like to be treated has lasted a lifetime.

In their place are what I simply call tips on living life to the fullest. Many are not new thoughts, while perhaps others are:

Read something every day, for reading stimulates the mind. Encourage your children to read in stead of playing video games. You say there is never anything in the newspapers but bad news? Then read a book of poems, the bible, or some other book that will comfort you or affirm you.

Volunteer or support a charity. For peace on earth and goodwill to all men is an attitude, not just mere words in a song sung once a year. Show that your compassion knows no bounds by making a commitment throughout the year, not just around the holidays. Simply adding two or three extra dollars to your utility bills each month will help someone else to have heat during the winter. I have done this for years.

I admit to being a sucker for pets. Every cat that has ever owned me has been a stray that appeared at my door. I guess they knew an old softie when they saw one. I donate money to tons of agencies to insure that Muffin or Fido is spayed and neutered and hopefully adopted out. The result of my generosity has been a lifetime membership in the Friskies Hall of Fame, and I have not bought birthday cards, Christmas cards or a calendar in years. But the thought of fewer animals being put to sleep soothes my spirit.

Remember good times and let go of the bad. Some of us wear old hurts like clothing everywhere we go. And we can recite every slight, real or imagined, verbatim. Until you let go of the past, you will never heal.

Prioritize. Pick out things that are important to you and let the others go for a while. Stay with one thing at a time and complete it instead of starting two or three and never finishing any of them.

Indulge yourself occasionally without feeling guilty. Take a few minutes just for you and do whatever it is that will calm you and relax you. Perhaps it's meditation or a few minutes walking on a treadmill. Take a hot bath instead of a quick shower.

Lastly, resolve to only doing the things that bring you happiness. Surround yourself with people that you like being around. Negative people or negative things should be avoided at all cost. Learn to laugh at life's absurdities instead of stressing out over them. I do this daily.

Someone once said that "Joy is not merely incidental to your spiritual quest, it is vital." So starting now, and for years to come, instead of lamenting the road not taken, strive to get some joy in your journey.

The Commandments According to Mother (Lessons for Living)

As a child I studied the Ten Commandments in Sunday school. You know: "Honor thy father and thy mother." "Thou shall not steal, covet thy neighbor, their ox or ass," etc. For a long time I never knew what covet meant, or that ass in that context was a donkey and not a curse word. But much like a tune that, once heard, you can't get of your head, were these lessons in living.

My mother, however, had some commandments of her own. Unlike Rorschach tests where every inkblot looked like a duck, the commandments according to mother were not open to interpretation. They simply were; 'thou shall not, don't, and stop that right this moment, you hear me?' So here is my take on them:

On dating:
If you lie down with dogs, you sometimes get up with fleas. This was a tip on safe sex, I think.

Economics 101
You must learn to save for a rainy day. Good girl that I was, I took this to heart. The next time it rained, I went shopping. Followed

by what I have personally found out to be a self-fulfilling prophesy: that a fool and his money are soon parted.

Economics 102

A penny saved is a penny earned. I say a penny saved means another penny that needs to be rolled up and taken to the bank–yet another chore for women. For my husband would rather die than roll up anything: coins, paper towels. Ignore that little ditty 'find a penny, pick it up, all day long you have good luck.' The last time I bent down to pick up a penny, I ripped my pantyhose. Good luck? I think not.

On Waste:

Waste not: want not. This was always at a meal of foods that consisted of liver or some other equally disgusting item, followed by "There are children in BiAfra who are starving." Only recently did I discover this place actually existed and was not a place she made up.

On Beauty:

Tuck in that lip or by all that is Holy, I will give you something to really stick it out for. Come to think of it, perhaps that wasn't a beauty tip.

On Respect for Oneself:

I still remember the time that a girl in my fourth grade class had a birthday party and invited all her friends I guess, so a couple of us weren't invited. Everyone talked about this party for days, including me. Somehow I guess I talked myself into an invitation. So the day before the event, an invitation appeared in our mailbox. I was so happy I didn't know what to do.

My mother however was not impressed. Several questions later revealed that the other children had received *stamped* invitations in the mail days ago. Needless to say she would not let me go. She said something that I'll never forget. It didn't make a lot of sense to me at the time. She said, "You are as good as anyone else. If you can't be the tablecloth, don't be the dishrag, for sometimes the dishrag gets thrown out with the dishwater." As a child I didn't appreciate how profound this probably was. I simply wanted to go to the party.

Other truisms followed. I grew up hearing that all you had to do was put your mind to something, and it could be achieved. If first you didn't succeed you tried and tried again. Forced to do chores around the house, we never feared that an 'idle mind was the devil's workshop.'

From my mother I learned that you were judged by the company you kept, and that no good deed ever went unpunished. By trying to keep up with the Jones, a fool and his money were soon parted. And while I didn't know every family who lived in our neighborhood when I was growing up, none I recalled were ever named Jones.

I learned that every 'cloud had a silver lining,' and that 'cleanliness was next to Godliness.' My elbows, knees, and neck, scrubbed with Ivory soap until they were nearly raw, paid homage to this mantra.

As an adult, I have finally gained an appreciation for my mother's wisdom. From it I learned early not to look to others for approval, but to rely on my judgement. I learned that negative people should be avoided at all cost, and that positive people help me to shine.

Today many of those sayings make sense. Still, I admit that that 'bird in a hand is worth two in bush' thing, I still don't understand. A bird in a hand today could turn around and peck your eye out. Now had she said, thou shall not covet thy neighbor's shoes, that I would have understood. But perhaps we are not meant to understand everything. Often some things just are. Isn't that just how it is sometimes with lessons?

Mr. Work With

I hear it all the time. Women friends talking about trying to find Mr. Right, many settling for Mr. Right Now, because he happened to be there at the moment. Tired of being alone, others pair up with Mr. Wrong and sometimes end up with Mr. Psycho. Their reasons for doing what they do are as varied as why they have so many shoes. They say that they are tired of going out with girlfriends. And that going places alone somehow screams *desperate.*

Some desire men who are unavailable both physically as well as emotionally. Many may have wives or are otherwise attached, or believe they are so head and shoulders above everyone else you wonder how they walk through doors without giving themselves a concussion. Others want someone who looks like Denzel or some other celebrity *'hottie,'* who is financially stable, walks and talks like the man in their fantasy, and will take them away from it all.

However I never hear these women speak about the 'average Joe.' The ones who may not dress, or act, walk or talk like the man in their fantasy. But he goes to his job every day. He never misses a day of work even when he may not be feeling his best. He may have a nice car or at least a car that runs. This man pays his bills on time, has some money in the bank. He adores his mother and sisters and treats them with love and respect. He will give his friends the shirt off his back if they need it. He may not be where he wants to be in life, but he is working hard to get there and would love to find a woman willing to help him.

Why is it that woman never talk about him, never seem to notice or even consider him in their dream when trying make a love connection? Even women who may not be all that they can be, have no education, or skills, or interests, or have anything to bring to the relationship table, want their men to have everything. Let's face it. Like many women, not every man is college material. Not every man is comfortable wearing a shirt and tie or tuxedo. Some men are better working with their hands, building things and creating things.

The play aunts and older women who made up my 'village' when I was girl always told me that it was fine to have a man with book learning and education. But they advised me to be sure that he also had 'motherwit'. Meaning that he should also possess good common sense, and have a way to 'make a way' when times were hard. So I always kept this in the back of my mind when I was dating.

I remember the first time I ever saw the man that I eventually married. I was sipping a Rum and Coke with a couple of friends on the air base where we were stationed in Idaho when the waitress plunked down four more drinks down in front of me. As I started to ask her if she thought that I was an alcoholic, she mentioned that a cute guy, who appeared to be heading toward the Exit sign when I looked, had bought them for me.

Out the corner of my eye I saw a guy wearing a brown two-piece 'pleather' (a blend of leather-look vinyl) suit and matching boots. You are probably thinking 'pleather'? However you must remember that this was the early 70's. I was actually happy that he was not wearing a red, black, and green suit, (the colors of Africa) with matching platform shoes, like the actors in those movies like "The

Mack" and "Superfly" for you will see that those flag-colored suits did exist.

Meeting him for the first time a couple weeks later, I asked him about all that liquor. He said that he had noticed me over at the table and had asked the waitress what I was drinking. And since he had to leave, he wanted me to buy my drinks so, hopefully I would be taken care of for the rest of the evening. What a nice guy, I thought. I can work with this. I didn't tell him that I had given all but one of the cocktails to my companions who drank anything if it was free.

During the dates that followed I learned that he had been in the Air Force about two years, joining right after finishing high school. And while he wore the brown suit and matching boots much too often for my taste (it was actually pretty nice), I discovered that he had goals and a plan for his life. He told me that he seeking his own Mrs. Right to help him to be all that he knew that he could be.

He was the man of my fantasy. He took me shopping and waited around patiently while I raced from store to store like a shopper on steroids. If I couldn't decide which outfit to buy (this happens more often than I care to admit), he encouraged me to buy them both or bought the one that I could not or would not buy. Most of all, he treated me the way I was taught that a man should treat me. Who knew that among the tumbling tumbleweeds of Idaho that I would find this diamond in the rough?

He possessed 'motherwit,' which came in handy as we tried to run a household after getting married. Between military paydays he shot pool, played cards, and shot baskets for money to tide us over, so that I could continue to send money home to help my mother. While some might consider this gambling, I knew that I had found a winner for he showed me that he would use whatever he had to ensure that I would always be taken care of, a promise that he made my mother.

71

Over the years, I have bought him some clothes. Not to try to change him but things that I knew would look good on him. Over the years he has taken enough classes for continuing education credits and several college degrees. But his natural intelligence and keen insight on so many things is what has stimulated me the past thirty years.

So I advise women not to miss out on their own diamond-in-the-rough for supposed riches. The movie star and the girl-next-door usually only happen in the movies. Give some thought to the single guy next door, the carpenters, painters, guys working on road crews and others who toil from sunup to sunset. For they may have something that is lacking in others but is truly more valuable in the long run. They may have a heart of gold.

Relationship Addict

Not one, not two, not three, but four relationships in 13 months. Is that too many a woman friend asked me recently as she was telling me how she seemed to be battling zero on the relationship Richter scale? Might I suggest some sort of Patch, I think? On second thought maybe what you really need is a relationship blanket. What I said was that only she could be the judge of that. After all, I have never been able to eat just one Lays potato chip, have bought four pairs of shoes at one time even though they were not on sale, so I might not be the best judge on all things in moderation. Still the answers to these simple questions may be a revelation for her and others floundering in the relationship love boat. So here goes:

1.   Are you constantly seeking love in all the wrong places, seeking nurturing from men who are either unwilling or unable to give it to you?

2.   Do you appear desperate for approval from the men in your life at the risk of setting aside your own thoughts and ideas?

3.   Do you accept treatment from a man that you would never accept from a woman?

4.   Do you act helpless around men?

5.   Do you flaunt your sexuality to get what you want from men?

6.   Do you have a humiliating history of believing everything

men tell you? If so, you may be a chronic relationship junkie.

After answering these you probably feel the urge to take to your bed (alone, please) with a pint of Ben and Jerry. But alas all is not lost. You CAN stop this pattern of behavior and regain control of your life. But in order to change you must start by asking yourself some tough questions: like why does this keep happening? What am I doing that attract these kinds of men? And how can I stop it?

We often harbor the impression that our experiences are unique, but women everywhere experience the same things, only the details are different. We have all suffered at least one horrible breakup, have juggled two boyfriends at the same time, praying that we don't call them by the wrong name. And how many of us have felt like failures when relationships ended? We ask ourselves what could we have done differently to make it work. Never mind that our partners did nothing to make it work either.

Still some women go through binges, dating anything that wear pants trying to prove that they are still desirable after a relationship disaster. They race from one relationship to another. So caught up in the race to find somebody, to get married, and maybe have a baby that they lose sight of other things like their hopes and dreams. They break up with a guy at breakfast and by that night they have made another love connection. They can't wait to give another guy all their numbers; home phone, cell phone, and pager. Deep in a martini fog and the dim lights in a club, girl he looked *good*, they say.

Many women like men to buy them things: gifts or groceries. When they break up, men want to take back the stuff that he has bought her. Others like men to give them money. Believe it or not, there are those who focus on the material things, often overlooking character flaws that are not shown until well into a relationship. Is this you? If so, heed this. Do not, I repeat, do not suffer disrespect for furniture and chicken. Buy your own.

Even when women see things about a man that they really don't like; he get angry when things don't go his way, he always shows up late whenever they have plans, he waits until receiving a second shut-off notice before paying bills, women hold on. Some women feel that having a man somehow validates them as a woman or even a person. They feel that it is better then having no one. They say no one is perfect.

Others are afraid of being alone for any length of time. Once they have cut off the television or stereo and hung up the telephone, they are forced to think about themselves, about relationships, and it frightens them. Truth is, at one time or another, we all find ourselves alone. If you were not born a twin, then you started out in life alone.

Women say that it is easy for me to talk, after all, I have a man. Well I have not *always* had a man. Like many woman there were times that I was alone, and lonely. I simply filled my life with other activities, so that a man or a relationship was not the *only thing* I focused on. It was then that men, and eventually the man who would become my husband, came into my life

Why not take a class that you may have always wanted to take? Take a trip or spend time with friends and family. The point is, get to know you. Figure out what you will accept in a relationship and what won't. You can do this. After all, short of a 12-step program, what have you got to lose?

The Change

I didn't ask for 'the change.' I volunteered for Scotch and steamy sex. But it's hard to feel sexy when you are sweating like a pig on a barbecue pit, but dry in places where you really need to be moist. There are the highs and lows that come from hormones going awry. And the unspeakable gymnastics you go through when putting on your pantyhose, like holding your breath and sucking in your stomach, then forgetting to breath again, causing yourself to nearly pass out.

When I was a girl, I often overheard older women talking about some friend of theirs who was going through 'the change.' "Girl, she's going through the change." They say, "You better not say nothing to her, or she's liable to curse you out!" Their whole tone of voice was different when they said this, and they made it seem so mysterious.

Children take things literally, so I found myself staring at the woman in question when she was around and wondering when she was going to change. I also speculated on what she might change into. I remember hoping that she would be a puppy and I could play with her, since my mother would not let me have a dog. And despite mother telling me it was impolite to stare at people, I still stared, like people watching an accident, I couldn't look away.

Nothing happened as far as I could tell. Except that the woman in question always seemed to be wiping her face. Sometimes leaving streaks of face powder from a well-used powder puff. The funny thing was that no one else was sweating. Back then I remember thinking I was never going through the change, whatever it was. If you couldn't change into something fun like a cat or dog or something else that was fun, why bother?

We have all read about the biological changes that takes place in a woman's body, the night sweats, the hot flashes that start at the top of your head and trickle downward, but what we don't often hear about are the other changes that are equally important. Like the emotional feelings, the depression, or the blues some women experience. The knowledge that they can no longer bear children, whether they really wanted to do this or not, affects many women's sense of self. And while young women are singing "Who let the Dogs, Out," others of us find ourselves screaming "Who turned the heat up?"

I am in the middle of this journey myself. Sure, I am still hot. It just comes in flashes now. And much like many things that we have little or no control over, I am learning to go with it. I am never without a tissue handy. And there are other changes as well. I have switched to nightgowns with snaps in the front for those times that my personal thermostat kicks on at 3:00am.

I heard someone say that getting older is a lot like having a baby, except you don't have anything to show strangers in the street. Still with the change, come wonderful opportunities for reinventing ourselves. It is a chance to do the things that we have always dreamed of doing. Things like travel around the globe, climb a mountaintop, wear your rubber flip-flops out in public. For me it was writing a book. I believe that it was F. Scott Fitzgerald who said, "American lives do have second acts." In my mind, all *great* productions do.

Fears

Fears of rejection, those
Demons of darkness
That forces us to repress thoughts
Once uttered, would
Reveal an imperfect you.
So we are held captive by
The quicksand of our
Insecurities
While all around us, others
Reach for the sun

LIFE
(OR SOMETHING LIKE IT)

One Soldier's Story

Unlike other little girls, I didn't aspire to being a doctor, lawyer, or Indian chief. I told people I wanted to travel and see the world, then maybe find and marry Mr. Right. I didn't care one whit whether my 'Mr. Right' was tall, dark and handsome. Okay, maybe the handsome part, and maybe tall, or just a little taller than me. But I knew that he would be a soldier. My father served in World War II and often entertained my sister and me with stories about his experiences, the people that he met, and all the places that he had been. So I suspect that's where this idea came from.

In my daydream I never pictured *myself* wearing a uniform. Yet there I was, years later, standing at attention in my blue uniform and little flight cap, answering the call to arms as an airman: a decision that left the tongues of the women who came to my mother's beauty shop clicking. For the life of them they couldn't understand why a 'nice girl like me *wanted* to be a soldier.'

They regaled me with horror stories of girls who had gone into service. There was Mrs. So and So's daughter who joined the Marines and came out 'funny' (gay). Another supposedly went in and came home pregnant. Forever dancing to my own beat, I went anyway, eventually finding myself the wife of a career airman–an all too familiar scenario of warriors leaving behind friends and family to defend the rights of others around the globe.

Still people are surprised when they find out that I spent over twenty years in the military. They say things like "you don't look like a soldier." What does a soldier look like I think? Out of uniform most of them look like regular people. Especially after Basic Training, when their hair is allowed to grow back after the scalping. They say, "Why, you don't look hard or anything, you look like ... well a lady." And I think that I am a lady, which didn't change despite hours spent marching in heavy boots. And they always want to know what made me join the service?

The truth is I joined the Air Force because of the uniform. There you have it. Thumbing through a magazine one day I came across an ad for the Air Force, and there was a picture of a beautiful African-American female in a crisp blue blouse with tab tie and navy skirt. She stood beside two other Airmen, another female and a handsome male, all looking in the camera with a poster behind them imploring the innocent to "Aim High, Join the Air Force."

Reflecting back sometime later I think I might have been drunk that day, although I don't know how as my mother never had liquor in our house. It could have been that hard apple cider though. That would explain my pulling out the post card that was underneath their picture and filling it out and dropping into the mail on a lark, which I did, and quickly forgot all about it. In fact, I think I might have been drunk my entire eight years on active duty, because it all seems like one big blur. You are probably thinking: and they let her carry an M-16?

From that day on my life flashed before my eyes. I took the military exam and passed. The recruiter in my area bought the test to my house. He kept telling me that the Air Force was the elite of all the military branches and that I was going to be a great asset to them. I would get a chance to travel the world and even go to college if that was what I wanted. Before I knew it, I was on an airplane winging to San Antonio, Texas to military basic training and to another world.

The Air Force really didn't knew what to do with me. After all, it was 1971 and ,according to military statistics, between 1948 and 1973 women in the service only made up about two per cent. My first permanent party base, Mountain Home Idaho, had 20 women when I arrived. Two more African-American females came a week after I did which meant that there were now nine African-American females. There was one Puerto Rican and the rest were Caucasian. There must have been over 300 men on the base. Some women would have thought that they had died and gone to heaven, except for the uniforms. I am not sure Heaven allows camouflage.

A Black Chief Master Sergeant who reminded me of my father headed the section in Base Supply where I was first assigned, so we bonded right away. I remember that he smoked cigars, and always carried a spare in his socks. And he drank Jim Beam. I drank my first shot of Jim Beam ever, two weeks after I met him. It burned a path straight down to my stomach.

Back then, my male counterparts fit into two categories in my life. They were the ones that I dated or the ones who appointed themselves as my guardians. At twenty years old and away from home for the first time, it was a role I accepted. While I earned a Marksmanship ribbon for shooting the M-16 in those early days in the Air Force, the military spent a lot of time trying to prove to us that we were still women. Our drills in marching were accompanied by lessons on relearning how to walk like a lady. With combat boots that was no easy task. Men opened the doors for me and let me walk ahead of them. I had always accepted this as a sign of courtesy and not an equality issue–nothing more, nothing less.

I was the only woman in the whole Civil Engineering Squadron when my husband and I were reassigned to an air base in South

Carolina. There were over 200 men in the squadron. Our Commander thought that was a hoot, so at Commander's Call (a monthly meeting) he would always ask me to stand, to show me off to the troops I suspect. Could this have been sexual harassment? Maybe, I don't know. I didn't feel threatened by it, nor offended.

The Air Force gave me the independence that I craved after leaving home, but with the structure that I needed. I was on my own; I had a roof over my head, money in my pocket, yet I was never alone. Eight years after joining I earned a bachelors degree. Two years later a masters, all courtesy of Uncle Sam. That alone was worth it.

And I did travel and saw a lot of the world. Granted, a couple of the locations, Idaho and South Dakota were more of the L.L. Bean travel variety. Still, how many women can boast that they got up close and personal to a buffalo? And I am not talking about the ones on the nickels rattling in your purse.

Still, to say that everything was perfect when I was in the service would be a lie. Yes, there were men who didn't believe a woman should be among them and let that be known every chance they could. Yes, there were men and women who were prejudiced, competitive, and simply mean-spirited. But you find that everywhere.

Yet, the self-confidence that I gained as well as the other skills I honed have been invaluable. The military took a frightened young girl and turned her into an accomplished woman and warrior. It was the best decision that I ever made for myself. And while the chances of being involved in combat are more real today than it was back in my day, I would do it again.

Reality Check

I don't know about you, but I am so tired of those so-called reality television shows. You know "Survivor," "Temptation Alley," "Fear Factor," and "Yes I AM Crazy and will Prove It for a Million Dollars," where men and women test their prowess in the jungle, under water, etc., seeking fame and fortune while turning otherwise decent people into voyeurs. These shows are getting more and more bizarre with television pushing the envelope in search of ratings. Where will they draw the line?

And what does it say about those of us who sit down night after night to watch, with our hands hovering over our eyes (or is that only me) as a man stands in the middle of a bunch of snakes. Or as we watch as a woman allows rats as big as house cats to crawl all over her? Some might say that she is simply playing with her food as we have all seen one or two of these shows where the rats ended up as dinner. .

While my husband watches a couple of them, I don't look at this stuff except when he asks me to come see some horrific, you-have-got-to-see-this-to-believe-it scene. Boy what we won't do for love. I have never seen "Survivor" I or II. I don't know, or even care, who Big Brother is. For anyone who has served in the military or worked for the federal government knows that Big Brother exists, and that he is everywhere.

Even the promos frighten me. That one of the person standing in the middle of a bunch of writhing snakes gave me chill bumps all the way down to my toes. Give me a good chick flick, a comedy or a mystery any day. A good show, in my opinion, would be Angela Lansbury of Murder She Wrote teamed up with Colombo and the doc on Diagnosis Murder to solve a murder about aliens in Wal-Mart. Now that would be something worth seeing.

Folks who need a dose of reality should come to some of our homes. For reality is sticking your hand in a sink full of greasy water as you try to unclog the kitchen sink with a Barbie plunger. Reality is experiencing a full-blown case of PMS without a Kit Kat bar in sight. It's the 'what can I fix quickly for dinner' saga, all the while your husband is waving a wrinkled shirt in front of your face. You know he is not fanning your fevered brow because one the cats has just coughed up a hairball the size of a ping-pong ball on your foot. At that moment you long for something to take you away, anything: an airplane, Calgon, Jack Daniels. For a taste of reality these same people might try being a single man raising his son by the 'walk tall but carry a big stick' motto when his boy's reality is a fifth grade classmate, crouched in a 'gangster lean,' carrying a 44 Magnum. Reality is trying to find pantyhose that fit.

To really test their survival quotient, these people don't have to brave the outback of Australia, or the jungles of Central America. They can simply try walking the streets alone after midnight in any inner-city USA. And if they really need something to beat their chest at and shout the battle cry, they could do something to make walking down those same streets safer.

For, in reality, the test of endurance is not eating rodents and living to tell about it. Why, even I have done that. Well, not a rodent actually. It was Octopus Tempura (a batter mixture) dipped and fried in Tokyo, Japan. I was told it was fish and was delicious. Actually it wasn't bad, just rubbery. Can you say tires in Japanese?

The true test of endurance is staring hatred, betrayal, and soul-deep pain in the face daily without flinching. It is being beat down by the injustice of man's inhumanity to man and the evil that they do. The prize is most certainly not a million bucks, a book, or even movie deal. The prize is that, after all is said and done, we are still standing.

Love Songs

Is it just me or do all rap songs sound alike? I am mainly talking about the ones sung by the guys. Still, I suppose if I understood the words I would like them better. Maybe. You've probably heard a few, for you can't help it if you listen to the radio. They all appear to be about the 'bling, bling,' the 'phat this' and 'phat that.' 'It's all about getting paid,' and someone threatening to go and get their 'gat.' 'Gat,' I learned from my godson, is a gun. I guess he could tell from the look on my face that I didn't have a clue what any of this was and needed an interpreter. And what kind of song is the 'Thong Song'? Who in their right mind would buy a song about panties?

You see, today's lyrics have no reality for me. Not true for the millions of teenagers and youth in our world today. Their choices seem to fall into two categories: where young girls know sex and disrespect before they know love, and where many young men seem to think that young girls are put on this earth for their pleasure or abuse.

When I was girl, the whole man/woman relationship thing could be summed up through 'ole school' lyrics. Back then music was the language that explored every facet of life. These were songs about people who worked hard, loved hard and still sometimes lost and taught us that life was precarious and that love was a rare, cherished, but often complex thing.

I will never forget the first time that I heard, the song "Me and Mrs. Jones" sung by the singer Billy Paul. It came on the radio one sunny morning as I dressed for work in my too-short-for-military-regulation skirt, and my black spit-shined pumps (yes some used real spit). This song nearly took my breath away as it spoke of lovers everywhere who met secretly in cafés and other out-of-the-way places. knowing what they were doing wasn't right according to the Good Book, yet unable to help themselves. It spoke to the essence of the human heart. Listening to it, you could not help but feel sad for relationships where people are caught in the middle of trying to love two.

Through the years, my life has been touched by the lyrics of so many singers. "Let's Straighten It Out," by Latimore, reminded me never to go to bed angry. While the late Barry White, truly the icon of love, helped many to resolve intimacy issues; for you could not help but be moved by his love songs. And now and again I still feel like "Getting down. Getting funky and Getting Loose" but hope that I don't get down and can't get back up.

More times than I care to remember I have forgotten that smiling faces sometimes only pretend to be your friend. And when I get sick and tired of turning the other cheek to the point that all I can think about is getting payback, instead, I give my problems up to a much higher authority to handle.

Not long ago as I sat in my car waiting for the light to change, a song by the Manhattans came on the radio. As I sang along with the words I was startled by the LOUD music from a teenager in a car next to me. He had the sound up so loud, it drowned out my music even though my car windows were rolled up and the air conditioner was on. Still I heard the profanity, as did everyone else around us. The teenager with his baseball cap on backward, bopping his head to the beat, seemed unfazed by it all.

"What's going on?" the late singer Marvin Gaye asked years ago. Many of us are still asking that question today. We are asking who will replace some of our most respected leaders who seem to be passing on daily? We are asking how is it that our children know the entire words to rap songs, but can't read "The Cat in the Hat" when we say that we are working hard so that no child is left behind?

"Who will save the children, save the babies?" Marvin asked. Who will tell them that they can make their own music by studying hard in school and staying away from negative influences, whether it's drugs, people, or music. For nothing sounds quite as sweet as the sounds of success. Or that the words "I love you" should never come after a black eye. Dear Marvin, you asked us these questions some thirty years ago. It's 2004 and we still have no answers, sadly only more questions.

Consider the Source

Have you ever noticed that there are people who can't wait to give you advice on whatever ails you? All right I admit, I tend to be one of them. Every illness and affliction that anyone mentions that they have, a headache, a toothache, or bloating, like water flowing from a faucet, all the remedies that have worked for me spills forth from my lips. Panties versus throngs, the great divide, Tylenol versus Midol for cramps. Liquid or pills, if only your throat could talk.

I think that it's a woman thing, for you hardly ever hear men advise each other on anything, except perhaps the merits of whether to *pour* beer on the barbecue while it's cooking, or to *drink* it while standing over the grill; BAM! shades of Emeril Lagasse: same principle, different procedure. You've never heard a guy suggest that you rub a bar of soap over a stubborn zipper, or argue whether hot wax or shaving is the least painful method of removing leg hair. Okay that last part I hope *never* to hear from a guy.

I admit some suggestions do work. For example, putting mustard on a burn does take the sting out. That is if you don't mind walking around smelling like a hotdog. And putting fresh greens like collards in a clean pillowcase and running them through a full cycle in your washing machine, I am told, cleans them well. It even breaks off the stems and everything, people say. This is wonderful if you are preparing greens for a lot of people. However I recommend that you forgo the detergent, bleach and Downy fabric softener. Unless you prefer that your vegetables be static-free and have that Rainwater Fresh taste.

People tell me that I look younger then I really am: bless them. I tell them that it is a combination of things: Scotch (whiskey), good genes, and 40-some years of washing my face with Noxzema medicated cream. My mother used Noxzema all her life and I started as a young girl. So even women who don't drink take both of these as an endorsement.

Still we have all had recommendations that did not pan out, or suffered serious fall-out from using them. That's why many professions require you to have a license. Many recall the hair relaxer that relaxed folks' hair so much that the hair fell out of their head. Now that's relaxed. I heard somewhere that one of the ingredients was potato. Is any wonder why I prefer my spuds, fried, french-fried or mashed?

Not long ago I was talking with a colleague in my office when another co-worker passed by my door. It was around Christmas, so there were only a few people at work in the whole building. As the co-worker poked her head in the door, my friend who was visiting admired a necklace that she was wearing. You know women will discuss clothing at the drop of hat, regardless of the original topic.

This woman told us that the beads were made of Myrrh, as in 'Frankincense and' from the Bible. She asked had we ever smelled Myrrh, to which I replied no. My other colleague hadn't either, which I was happy to hear, as I didn't want to appear uncouth for being the only one in the room who hadn't smelled it.

The woman then told us that over the years the Myrrh scent had disappeared. However, *someone* suggested that if she wet the necklace the smell would return. Well, she said that she wet it, but, much to her horror, all the beads stuck together in one long clump. She ended up having to re-string the whole thing.

Once my colleague and I stopped laughing we congratulated her on a job well done. But before she could finish her story, both of us asked her if she had checked out that store in the malls that sells fragrances to see if they carried Myrrh. I know, I know, we couldn't help ourselves.

I have even tried that *Zen* thing of biting my tongue, but it doesn't help. For the instant the pain subsides, I find myself giving someone advice on what to use, for say that fungus on their big toe. While a few folks do relish telling others stuff that may not be good for them, my idea is to help, not harm.

Still common sense dictates that if a person with no hair recommends a great hair product, unless you are bald or that is the look that you have been contemplating, you might wish to pass on that. With every action, we know that there is a reaction. You can't hide from the world or be afraid to live life. So go ahead try new things. But stop a moment, you know, and consider the source.

Where is Your Hat?

As I dress for church today, I can still hear my mother's voice as though it was yesterday. She, like so many women her age, felt that you covered your head in reverence in the Lord's house. Many of us remember getting a new hat for Easter when we were young, along with a new dress, coat and maybe new shoes. There we were, dressed in our little white patent-leather shoes and little white socks with our hair curled. Perhaps it was braided with a 'Chinese Bang' kissing our foreheads with that little straw hat plunked on top. I don't know where the term 'Chinese Bang' came from because I know some Chinese and I have never seen them wearing a bang like I wore.

Historically hats were worn to emphasize the rank and importance of the wearer; examples being hats worn by military members, the biretta worn by priests, and the scholar's mortarboard. During the Middle Ages, religious practices based on the teachings of the New Testament required women to cover their hair completely, both indoors and out, so I suspect that this where my mother got this idea.

No one in my opinion however, can wear a hat like African-American women. It's more of an attitude than anything else, and Sundays are banner days for wearing them. This is the day hat wearers strut their stuff front and center in their topped facades. Right before your eyes will appear a fashion-show of flocked, feathered, and face-framing styles running rampant. There goes a cloche style hat that borrows its cues from the 1920's flapper era, its dainty fit and trim crown worn close to the head. There goes a woman wearing a lampshade hat that resembles the fixture for which it is named. This hat is sometimes draped, or flocked and made of either velvet or wool. The pillbox is another popular style as is the fedora that is often worn tilted to the side.

Those longing for the limelight might sport any of these styles, covered in mesh, rhinestone starbursts or oversized horsehair bows. They might be draped in satin, trimmed in animal fur or braid or a whole field of daisies or some other flora and fauna. Still the real head turner is the woman sporting a hat made of hackle feathers looking like some giant bird about to take flight right before your very eyes. Caw, Caw! Where, oh where are the hat police when you need them? And it never fails that one of these hat wearers will take the seat in front of you at church or at a concert where you court whiplash from peeking through feathers or lace, your eyes blinded by rhinestones.

I was about twelve when a lady who worked with my mother gave her a bag of clothes that her children had outgrown. With money being tight and never one to waste anything my mother, thankful for this kindness, took them. Among these items were two hats. Both were sort of off-white in color and one had a veil that fell across the front.

My mother thought that they were nice. She didn't ask my opinion, so I offered none. Still since I was the oldest she thought that I should get the one with the veil. Now, any other time my sister who is five years my junior would have complained about something; my piece of chocolate cake was bigger than hers was, my dress was prettier, our mother loved me best, you name it. I noticed that she didn't ask for the hat with the veil.

So, off I went to Sunday school wearing with my hat with the veil, worn over my 'Chinese Bang' when something terrible happened. Out of nowhere came a breeze that blew my hat complete with veil right off my head. In the confusion that followed, it somehow came to rest in a mud puddle where somehow I stomped on it. My mother couldn't figure out how in the world that happened. I believe that it was a miracle, myself.

Still, there is nothing quite like wearing a hat that conjures up that image of true elegance and sophistication. For a properly worn hat can seemingly transform a person, even make them appear more youthful than they are. And wearing a hat can sometimes bring people luck as demonstrated above.

Today as I dress to go to church or someplace special, with my Fedoras matching the color of my outfit slanted just so, I think of my mother long gone. And I am reminded that there is just something about a hat, and about miracles.

Circle of Women

Growing up my mother always warned me that "women are not be trusted as far as you can throw them." Reflecting back, I suspect this is one of the reasons why I have often shied away from women's friendships. Through the years I did discover too late that a few were not trustworthy or worthy of my friendship. Still, you can not know betrayal until you have been betrayed.

To make a friend you must first be a friend, or so the old saying goes. And Lord knows that I have tried for I value friendships. I have listened to other women's tales of woe. I have clucked my tongue in all the right places and empathized. I have nurtured confidences, even dispensed tissues, tea and crumpets. Well, the crumpets were really Hostess Twinkies. But last week I read that Betty Crocker now makes crumpets. Perhaps I will get some the next time that I go shopping

With my poor track record with women, I usually preferred men friends to women friends. For once boundaries were established these relationships worked for me. Still I longed for the friendship that women can only get from other women. That sacred bond of kindred spirits, that stems from a commonality of shared experiences, like letting them see us in our shabbiest underwear while trying on clothes, our genuine affection and sense of trust. But rather than go through a lot of drama, I kept my distance.

So much to my surprise, it has taken me nearly fifty years to find my circle of women. Through them I enjoy what I call random acts of friendship. Like being asked to help decorate for the reception when a friend's daughter got married. How had she known that not having a daughter of my own, helping with this was something that was close to my heart? Two other friends also helped. One with the seating the 200 guests at the reception while another made the flower arrangements and decorated the alter in the church. All of us delighted in the sharing in the age-old custom of women in a village coming together to help with a marriage and the feasting.

Next there was the friendship cake. With a batter that is already started, a small portion is given to others to make their own pastry. As I kneaded the dough that was a big part of the process, I felt honored to have been included in this ritual especially after my friend explained the significance behind it. As I continued to knead, I thought of the woman who had shared it with me. I thought of how much I admire her and her commitment to her husband and family. I thought of her laughter, her enveloping smile and warmth that I had been the recipient of on many occasions as we worked on a project together. There was a Zen-like quality to the kneading process that I found soothing, for the more I kneaded the more relaxed I became.

When I broke my ankle some time back, women at work were wonderfully supportive. They helped me to navigate the hallways without bumping into walls the short time that I was bound to a wheel chair and later when I was on crutches. They ran errands for me, held doors, and did many things to keep my spirits up. I am certain their kindness hastened my recovery and for that they have my undying gratitude and friendship.

When I think of the many acts of friendship, and of the women who today are a huge part of my life, I am humbled by their unconditional love. These women who possess tremendous strength, poise, and exude this wonderful zest for life accept me for who I am. They are my sisters, my dream sharers and, wise beyond their years, they are my importers of wisdom. Their chosen life's work is a testament to their love of community and cultural pride. We cheer each other in our accomplishments while allowing each other the freedom to grow without losing our individual voices.

As I reflect on the wonder of it all I do so with the realization that a woman's rite of passage is a major growth experience. As human beings we are fragile creatures, once bitten, we are not simply twice, but often thrice shy. Still, lately I have come to realize that the shield that I hid behind, instead of being protecting, may have in actuality been alienating.

I'm Okay

They say that life is a journey, and boy do I have the bunions to prove it. Ask any woman and they will say that male disorder is rampant. While men pray for peace in the Middle East, women everywhere pray for the strength not to strangle the men we love. Stroll into anyone's house and you are likely to encounter chaos with the man of the house armed with a remote in both hands, challenging you and anyone who questions that as a character flaw, as being crazy themselves.

I can relate to this because I married a television nut. I discovered it quite by accident a few months after the honeymoon. There I was a 'brick house': thirty-four, twenty-five, thirty-six, standing in my birthday suit in front of the television, all fresh from my shower, smelling of Avon's MoonWind perfume, when he tried to peer around me to see the Buffalo Bills and some other football team pound each other into the ground. Please tell me for I don't understand how can he sit by and watch ten or twenty 300 pound men knock themselves silly, and a clogged sink nearly brings him to tears?

Other things drive me crazy. Like he can't understand why I am so ticked off by the shock of cold water hitting my bottom when I have gone to the restroom in the dark. After all I was trying to be courteous by not cutting on the lamp and disturbing his rest. Although my loud curse woke him up anyway. I know, I know according to Feng Shui, stress upsets my chi. But hey, my chi is not too happy with him right now either, and refuses to get involved in *my* drama. I now have a night light in the restroom and more often than not he remembers to put the seat down.

And how can he say that shopping *is* not a sporting event? While there usually aren't any hotdogs or beer at the stores where I shop, there is sometimes shoving, and in-your-face contact when there is only one pair of red pumps with the gold tip on the toe in a size 8 left in the whole place. There are hi-fives when the successful contender is left standing with the prized shoes. And no, we don't slap each other on the backside, in case anyone is wondering. A 'you go girl' is usually sufficient, thank you.

Yes and no are *not* good answers to questions particularly when the question is: "Does this outfit make me look fat?" Take it from me. No should always be followed by additional compliments. For example, "no baby, that dress makes you look like a million bucks." This is what we like to hear.

And don't say that *nothing* is wrong when we ask. We know when something is wrong. You should know by now that we are not going to let up until you tell us. And don't get mad at us if we keep pestering you. Because had you just gone ahead and told us what was wrong when first asked, we could have discussed it, maybe found a solution and have been finished with it by now.

Lastly don't tell us stuff unless you have all the information. For this drives us crazy. For example:

"You know Jim and his wife are separating." (We both know Jim)
"Really, what happened?" I ask.
"I don't know what happened I didn't ask him all that." he answers.

"Well how did he happen to tell you this? What were you doing?" I ask.

"We weren't doing anything, he just mentioned it." he replies.

"Where is she now, is she still living in the house?" I ask.

"I don't know, I didn't want to get all in the dude's business." he replied, with censure in his voice now indicating that he is finished with this even though he has really told me nothing.

I shake my head thinking why the heck he even told me this since he doesn't know anything. Now I am going to have to call around to some of our other friends and find out what's what. Like I don't have enough to do. I have a mind not tell him what I find out. That'll fix him.

This happens, I suspect, in even the most loving relationships. So ways on how to survive our relationship and my marriage has become my saving grace. Every day brings some new challenge. But I have learned from experience that if I focus on the things that drive me crazy, I will go crazy. So instead I try to take the high ground and draw what some call the line of demarcation, a strategy that successful relationships sometimes called compromise.

I won't nag him about sports, if he does not nag me about shopping. And as I pick up his dirty socks where they are actually *kissing* the clothes hamper, but didn't quite make it all the way inside, I just keep repeating, "I'm okay, but he has some serious issues."

.

Great Men
(and the Women behind Them)

They say that behind every great man, there is a woman. This is usually said flippantly in conversations right along with statements like "the road to hell is paved with great intentions," and that "it takes two to tango." Yet history has proven this to be so. For behind Napoleon, there was Josephine, behind Roy Rogers was Dale Evans and the list goes on.

While we are all familiar with Rudolph and Santa's elves, women knew that there had to have been a Mrs. Claus. Who do you think cleaned up behind those reindeer and provided directions so that boys and girls might receive their presents before say, Easter. For while Rudolph supposedly had a red nose, he did not have 'On-Star.'

Who is this woman behind the man? Often she is his mother, a woman moved by the resilience of the human spirit. A person who often stared into the face of hatred and racism, all the while refusing to be consumed by it. A person where phrases like 'thinking outside the box' was not part of her lexicon. Her reality most likely was getting little Johnny out of a box that contains cereal, when he decided that this was where he and the family cat would live.

She is a wife continuing where his mother left off. Largely invisible, adapting to a life that no way resembles her own master plan. Her dreams of pursuing law or discovering distant galaxies are now overshadowed by the needs of her husband and family. She often works not one, but two 'Mac' jobs to help put her husband through medical school or law school.

She is a woman trotting the globe behind a man whose uniform identifies him as a soldier. A woman crying silently while sewing on stripes, her tears falling upon deaf ears in a system that believes that if 'Uncle' had felt that a soldier needed a wife, he would have provided him with one along with his dog tags. Or perhaps she wears a blue uniform or green one of her own to work daily with full knowledge that service to her country could mean paying the ultimate sacrifice.

She is a woman whose husband's mistress has names like B1-Bomber stamped on her backside instead of some designer's label. Who at the slightest caress of his hands, hums and performs, earning him names like Top Gunn or Killer Joe. She is a woman who bears her babies alone in countries where rice is often more plentiful than formula. And the Gerber baby's face peeks out from words she can't pronounce. Would her commitment to this man always mean sacrifice on her part?

But the woman behind the man believes that the Lord is the strength of her life. And that belief helps to relieve her loneliness and fear. It helps every time the phone rings late at night, where she wonders if this will be the call where she will *know* what it feels like when a human heart breaks. Yet with enormous strength and character, she remains a faithful steward upholding the duties charged to her with dignity, knowing that the day will come when it will be her turn to sprout wings and soar.

As has been our practice the past thirty years my husband I review our original dreams to see how much of it we have accomplished, and those that still live on. At the end of this review he credits me for all that we have accomplished together. While I am humbled by his praise, the one constant that has always remained has been our commitment to each other and our life together. Like many men, whether they admit it or not, he agrees that without women holding up part of the sky, there would probably be fewer successful men.

It Took a Village

When Hilary C. wrote a book on this subject a few years ago you would have thought she had come up something truly profound. In my mind's eye I envisioned heads bobbing up and down and folks saying "amen sister" and "speak the truth and shame the devil" as if they were in church. Well, this concept is nothing new to me and people my age. For without question I am indebted to the women who watched over me when I was growing up. The teachers who took time out from teaching to listen to a child's tale of woe, and the women who we called our 'aunts' not because we were related by blood but as a symbol of our esteem and respect.

There was Mrs. Chestley* our elderly, neighbor who lived next door to us in Washington, DC. Sitting on her porch in the summer with her chewing tobacco or snuff as it was sometimes called and the can that she spit in regularly to the disgust of us kids, she kept her eye on the neighborhood and us. Sometimes her aim was off when she spit, and she sometimes missed my foot by mere inches.

Passing her house and speaking always got us a rundown on her endless aches and pains. "Oh honey, my arthritis is really acting up something fierce today," she'd say. "And so are my hemorrhoids," she'd continue. Too much information I remember thinking but was not crazy enough to say out loud. "Who was that boy I saw you talking to today? Who are his people?" she would ask without giving me a chance to answer. "You stay away from those boys for they only want one thing you know." Then she would hock and spit!

This one-sided conversation seemingly went on for hours while I waited patiently for her to finish. So one time I decided to by-pass this conversation when my sister and I walked past her house. When we got close we pretended like we didn't see her as we ran yelling and screaming in our play. Mrs. Chestly told my mother that we didn't speak, and we were scolded for being disrespectful to our elders.

Mrs. Jamison* was another neighbor. She took in foster kids, which explained why there were always different ones at any given time calling her mother. Mrs. Jamison was a whole village by herself. Not because of all the children that came and went, but because she was a gossip who often embellished her gossip upon the telling. She once lied on me about boys, (what else) to my mother. And when my sister and I tried to tell mother that she had lied, she didn't believe us for parents never liked to admit that, like children, grownups also lie.

Still whenever I read stories in newspapers and magazines about the collapse of the American family, I think back on my own web of protection and realize that people of today could learn much from the people I knew. The people of color, the aunts, and grandparents who took in orphaned relatives without monetary support, raised and nurtured them along with their own children. Their adoption process was less about formality, or the mumbo-jumbo of some attorney, but more about love and the power of prayer.

For these were folks who committed themselves to being part of our inner circle. Individuals who knew even back then what we are just finding out today, that the lack of mentors is often a barrier to success. These individuals recognized that it indeed took a village to raise a child, so they willingly chose to be a part of my family, my village, 'my people.'

*Names are ficticious, and do not reflect real people

Just Browsing,
Not Buying Anything

I used to have girlfriends who bought outfits, wore them to an event and then returned them the next day to the store for a refund. They made up all kind of excuses: when they got the dress home, the color was different than what it looked like in the store; that blouse made their skin color look washed out under regular lights; they didn't really like it after all once they got it home, etc. I could never do that. No, it's not that I am a goody two-shoes, or think that I am above that. The truth is that I am too clumsy. I just know that I would spill something on it, perspire so much that the outfit would be drenched from the armpits all way down to the hem and there is no way that I could pull that off. Anyway for some reason I just hate taking things back.

When shopping around for a man, I think that women should test out the merchandise before getting coupled up. After all, we squeeze the Charmin when no one is looking, although most of us won't admit to it. We thump away at melons to test their ripeness, although as hard I thump, I have still been on the receiving end of a melon that was not as sweet or good as I thought. We nibble strawberries, cherries, and grapes before buying them, telling ourselves that we are just testing them to see if they are any good before we buy them and them decide not to. Today I have heard that you can now be arrested for stealing if you are not planning on buying these items, but are simply filling up to keep from passing out while grocery shopping, so I have stopped doing that.

We test perfume by spraying some on our wrists, which of course has not always been the best thing for me. For I have this tendency to try out different ones and the combination that has resulted, ends up smelling like bug spray that even bees would be afraid to sting me for fear of catching something from me, like death.

Why we wouldn't ever buy a pair of shoes without first trying them on, for we know that a size eight from PayLess can fit differently from an eight from AJS Shoes. And we have to see what they look like on our feet from every angle possible. That's why they have those floor mirrors in the shoe department. Sure, some women experience impulse shopping, buying outfits or jewlery as a temporary fix for whatever is ailing them. I have done it myself. But that is not the best way to shop.

At this very moment, a woman somewhere is lamenting that she should not have gotten mixed up with the person she is with. Perhaps she wishes that she had spent more time *listening* to him when he said that he wasn't ready for a commitment. Instead of thinking that she could change his mind. After all, he has not seen all she has to offer, that *she is different from any of the other women he has dated.* Every strand of hair on her head is *real*; she has several degrees, has her own place, and has traveled all over the world. How could he not want her?

Somewhere another is doing all the things a wife does, buying him stuff; clothes, rings, watches, etc. She is cooking for him, keeping dinner warm when he gets in late, perhaps even doing his laundry when she does hers, and a host of other things. This man is probably thinking hey, if I can get all this PLUS discover of some Victoria's racier secrets from a girlfriend, why do I need a wife? Stop being so accommodating and demand more balance in the relationship. In other words, stop doing so much for a man hoping that he will choose you over another.

Instead of trying to change a man's mind or trying to force some sort of commitment from every guy that they date, maybe women should just simply date. Really get to know the guys that you go out to dinner or a movie with. Get past the outside appearance, the SUV, the designer labels and other material things. For once, you be the one to decide whether he fits all of your needs, emotionally, spiritually, or otherwise. Men have been doing it for centuries. You be the one to decide whether or not he is a keeper. And do it before investing a lot of time and emotion. In other words, try him on size. For in relationships much like shoes, one size *does* not fit all.

Murphy's Law

Why is it that every time that we women think that we've 'got it going on,' something will happen to convince us that this is not the case? For example, you are invited to a special event. You find the perfect outfit. You get your hair done and your eyebrows arched. You get a pedicure and a French manicure with the tips painted white. Nibble a couple of pieces of French toast, one or two French-fries and you are all set if you ever get to France. The morning of the event, you wake up to discover that it is your time of the month, and I don't mean payday, which we would prefer. It's Murphy's Law; if anything can go wrong, by golly it will.

Or how about when you are wearing a pair of slacks that are fitting just right? They caress your hips and thighs all in the right places. You are so in love with the way you look that nobody can tell you a thing when you feel something scratching you only to glance down and find that a dryer sheet is peeking out of one leg just as you are walking past a good-looking guy who is checking you out.

It goes on and on. You are wearing a polyester knit pantsuit on a warm day while sitting in a wooden chair. When you get up look around your seat to make sure that you have not left any of your belongings, you notice that there is a small sweat stain on the seat, validating what your man meant when he remarked, "Girl, you got a furnace down there."

Unlike other factions, Murphy's Law is the one true equalizer for no female is immune. As not long ago one of my co-workers discovered that upon her arrival to work that she was wearing two different shoes. They were both taupe and really not that much different in style. Still it bothered her to no end, so she stayed at her desk most of the day, hoping that no one would notice. That morning she had even worn a scarf to match her outfit, so you *know* that she thought that she was a fashion diva.

Then there was the day that my supervisor wore two different earrings on the same ear. Granted today wearing six earrings in one ear tends to be the norm, but this was a little different for her. First they were the dangling kind, which she rarely wore. Come to find out, one of the earrings had hooked itself to another. However, since they were in the same color family, I just assumed that she was making some sort of fashion statement.

Unfortunately, I too continue to have run-ins with Murphy's Law. There was the time that I was invited to my goddaughter's going-away luncheon when she decided that practicing criminal law was well, criminal, and decided to pursue another kind. That morning while nibbling a toasted bagel with jelly, a tiny drop of jelly fell on the mango blouse that I thought made may face glow. Fortunately my breasts were there to catch it, for who knows where the jelly would have ended up? During lunch I spilled water on my blouse. The jelly was lonely. Then the woman on my left spilled food on herself, as did the one right across from us. She, however, seemed annoyed when I told her that she had spilled food on her eyeglasses that hung from a chain around her neck. I suspect she had planned to save it for later, but I blew that by telling her. My Bad! By the end of the meal we had decided to form a club for women who should never leave home without a bib and are not ashamed to admit it.

Another time, upon getting up from my desk at work, I discovered that I had my slacks on inside out. Nobody told me. I only realized it when I happened to glance down and noticed the wide seams where they are sewn together were showing. By now it was 3:00 in the afternoon. Thank goodness I didn't have any meetings that day and had spent much of it in my office.

For the most part these things are harmless, only embarrassing. The confident me longs to take it in stride. However, the crazy woman who lives inside of me thinks that it is some kind of conspiracy dreamed up by men. I try to tune her out. I tell myself that the things that happen to me can happen to anyone. I keep telling myself this. It keeps me sane.

Keeping it Real

How many times have you heard someone utter the phrase "I'm just keeping it real?" There have even been songs written about it. But what does that mean? Does 'keeping it real' mean that I should stop wearing make-up and show my naked face to the world? If I should see Denzel in Kroger, so what? After all even *he* must realize that outside of Hollywood, most people do not come by that flawless complexion without Botox or some other help.

Curious, I asked the women at my beauty salon. Not surprisingly their responses were as varied as their professions. One said that keeping it real to her meant staying on track. It meant being bold and balanced. I took this as being more of a professional reality as this friend recently was promoted to the highest position that a woman has ever held in her company. She also felt that keeping it real meant keeping spiritually connected which frequently has been her source of strength.

'Keeping it real' for another appeared to be more relationship focused. This was evident when she indicated that when dealing with men, women should obey the rules of gambling: knowing when to hold them, knowing when to fold them, and knowing, not just when to walk away girl, but to run. In keeping it real she also believed that success was truly the best revenge.

Still, how can you keep it real, when all around you people and things are changing? We have more gadgets then we know what to do with and many of us are working longer hours to purchase them. We have voice-activated telephones in our cars, hand-held computers and cell phones that can snap your picture. Why you need this I'm still not certain. I am not buying one of them until someone creates one that takes off pounds from my image.

Everything is instant this or instant that. But we still do not have enough hours in the day to do everything. Our health is suffering and our children are running amok. So, we buy them cell phones and pagers so that we can keep tabs on them. We enroll them into every program, every class, so their palm pilot is filled with more play dates and appointments than your own.

How can you keep your head on straight when all around you people seem to be losing theirs, we think? Alas there are no simple answers. There is no magic pill that we can take to make these issues disappear. And try as we might, we cannot jog, or eat, drink or sleep our way out of this reality.

I look at my own life. I am educated and well traveled. I am blessed with a wonderful husband and home. While I am not rich by any means; I am making more money today than my parents ever imagined in their lifetime. I am rich beyond measure with friends. I give back by contributing to charities, through mentoring young people, and other good deeds. And while every now and then I buy something with a designer label, I still shop at Wal-Mart. At all times I try to be myself

Still, am I doing enough to 'keep it real' I wonder? I *think* so. But just in case, on my way home from work today I'd better stop off at Rita's Nail Salon and Rib Shack. As that's keeping it real.

I've Finally Got My Mind Together, But Now the Rest of Me Is Falling Apart

That phrase that goes, "a mind is a terrible thing to waste" could have been coined by my mother if someone else hadn't beat her to it. For my mother didn't believe in wasting anything, not one's mind, surely not one's cauliflower. In her opinion 'waste not' should have been one of the commandments, right there between that one about coveting stuff. She used to say that an idle mind was the devil's workshop, so to avoid that pitfall, she introduced my sister and me to doing chores around the house and to books forging a lifetime of reading and cleaning.

As a child I read all kinds of things from mysteries to the bible. I particularly loved the stories in the bible about people who overcame challenges like Daniel and the Lion's Den, Samson and Delilah and David and Goliath. After that incident I heard that there was a ban on slingshots.

Initially I began reading books for the great stories and for the hours of escapism they provided as I turned page after page. Then I began to read them for content and analyze them. Like Henny Penny, I discovered that if you want something done right, you usually have to do it yourself. Anyone who has a husband or children knows this to be true. From Romeo and Juliet I learned that a serious 'Love Jones' can sometimes be the death of you.

Homer's Odyssey, to me, was one of man's most poignant sagas. It's a story about the frailties of life, about a man trying to reclaim his fatherhood after years of wanderlust. It's about a wife longing for her husband, and finally about a son, searching for his long-lost father. Homer's Odyssey gave us our first glimpse of the absent-father syndrome.

In college I discovered Socrates and Plato. One scholar described Socrates as the man who looked upon the soul as the seat of working consciousness and moral character. I absorbed Nietzsche into my pores like steam, while Jung helped me to get in touch with my inner-child. Their thoughts twirled around and around in my head until I was dizzy, as I sought a higher consciousness while navigating passage into adulthood.

Today I read books for which they are intended. I read them for entertainment and sometimes enlightenment as I no longer feel the need to impress others with all that I know. But while I have finally got my mind together, the rest of me is going to pot. My thighs rub together when I walk, while my knees are in competition to see which one can crack the loudest. There's a whole lot of activity going on under my clothes, none of which can be described as foreplay. Still, I try not to let these things bother me. For I have found the courage to simply be. I am grounded. I am centered, finally.

Stockings,
The Saga Continues

For my 31st anniversary I am not requesting another diamond, tennis bracelet or some other token of affection. What I want is pantyhose that do not bind me in the crotch, run only on one leg and threaten to cut off the circulation to my waist. What *do* you do with a dozen pairs of pantyhose with one good leg women ask? Besides using them to buff your leather pumps? Try that, it works beautifully.

If you buy the same shade all the time, you simply cut off the bad leg of two pairs, snip the waist-bands so that you can still breath and walk at the same time, then slip on both pairs the same as you did just one. Sometimes you can wear these for several days if you put them on while wearing oven mitts.

I was around twenty when stockings became *hose* for me. It happened as was I shopping in a department store in Idaho where I was stationed with the military. Idaho, with its dust storms and tumbling tumbleweeds, was my reward for surviving eight weeks of basic training on my hands and knees scrubbing grout from bathroom tile with a toothbrush. Obviously the military felt I had not suffered enough.

While nicely dressed, this saleslady, who looked as if she had sucked on a lemon, inquired if she could help me in that nasal tone some salesladies use. Standing proudly in my blue uniform, I asked her where I might find stockings. "Stockings?" she asked in that nasal tone that was starting to grate on my nerves. "Yes stockings" I replied pointing to my legs. "Oh you mean *hose*," nasal nose said, and proceeded to sash-shay down the aisle leaving behind a cloud of Chanel Number 5 or one of its fragrant sisters, Chanel numbers 6 or 7.

As the military base was fifty miles away I bought various types of hosiery that day. I bought regular hose, pantyhose, and knee-highs. The hose that I bought required a garter belt, which I also had to buy, as I did not own one. Of course, to 'nasal nose', a woman not owning a garter belt was an affront to womankind everywhere.

One pair of knee-highs turned into the 'knee-highs from hell' with one leg that constantly fell around my ankles. One pair of pantyhose stretched so much I had to tuck the toe about three inches underneath my foot, inside my shoe. This made it feel like I had a pebble or something in my shoe every time I took a step.

Like so many women, I have resulted to strange measures to stop my hose from running. I keep nail polish handy at all times. Once I even resorted to an old wives tale of putting a package of hose in the freezer for a few minutes. Someone told me that the cold temperature toughened the fabric. This worked until one day, upon opening the freezer, my husband discovered a package of pantyhose embracing his T-bone steak. He immediately started calling around to mental hospitals to see if they would accept me.

Still, all this causes me to ponder. Men are now walking on the moon, while others are ordering their underwear dot.com. Yet no one has come up with hose that we women can wear more than once. Go figure.

Girls' Night Out

Some time ago, I had occasion to have dinner with a group of women whom I admire. We met at a Japanese restaurant in Washington, DC while there on business. One of the friends, a physician, was to receive a prestigious award on Capitol Hill for her work with asthmatic inner-city children, and the dinner turned into kind of a roast in her honor.

The meal began with laughter. I know I laughed when I saw the prices on the menu, and again when I was asked to select a wine to accompany our meal. Now I consider myself to be fairly sophisticated, although this being an upscale restaurant, with separate wine lists no less, I did not see any of my old stand-bys: Glen Ellen, Boone's Farm, or Ripple.

With the help of the friend sitting to my right, I decided what the heck, I would just pick a Sauvignon Blanc. So we selected a name we both liked and could pronounce, Spring Valley. We drank three bottles. It was either quite good or we didn't care as the night was young and we were poised for celebrating friendships.

Giddy perhaps from the wine hitting our empty stomachs, we selected our meal from entrees too numerous to believe. Like the twin sea bass arranged head-meeting tail on a plate circling a rice medley. Or the pork medallions grilled to perfection that were caressed by a fruited sauce and joined in marriage with herb-mashed potatoes. After all, my dinner companions, all accomplished women in their fields and world travelers, were used to most types of foods. Why I myself once ate Squid tempura in Japan and am still alive to talk about it.

After a couple more glasses of Spring Valley, one of my friends finally realized that the woman who stared back at her blatantly wearing the same outfit that she wore, was actually her own reflection in a mirrored wall. Our giddiness changed to outright laughter. Tonight was our night. Tomorrow we would applaud our friend on getting a taste of the recognition she so richly deserved.

Then we would return to our real lives. A couple of us would balance our checkbooks to decide which bills to pay first that month, or at all. Another would ponder whether she would be able to pay her daughter's medical school tuition come fall. Yet another would worry about the company budget restraints, wondering how long she would have enough money to continue to employ staff to do the work that still needs to be done.

All of us, upon returning home, would check to see that, while it was never level, the playing field had not shifted too much in our absence. And we all vowed to continue to work full-time battling racism and sexism, all the while keeping one eye out for the knives aimed at our backs.

While our diversity was obvious to even the most casual observer, what could not be seen was the common thread that bound us together, that thread of humanity, the thirst for justice and what is right. Because we have learned to keep them buried, they don't see the battle scars of fighters sometimes down, but never, ever, out. These things could not be seen by the naked eye.

But tonight, we would push this all aside. We would toast to friendships, to sisterhood, and to each other. We would toast the young waiter turned cameraman. We would toast the twin sea bass, and the lavender ice cream. And while we all agree that we must do this again soon, I hoped that we would. For one of the pitfalls of success is often overlooking important, meaningful things like the special bond and support that women often receive from each other. For when one of us gains recognition, we all win. However tonight, we are simply who we are, girls/women out on the town.

Sharing Confidences

Yesterday I overheard a friend
speaking to another in confidence
That she sometimes
Feels invisible in her own home.
It's not maliciousness on his part she says,
But more like indifference
As she competes with the remote control,
And with his secret thoughts
that she is afraid to question
For she knows from past experience
That once secret thoughts are revealed,
two things must happen
You must act upon it, or you do nothing.
She states this matter-of-factly, as if resigned to it,
So, because I am not supposed to know,
I sit quietly by and watch
While pieces of her soul crumble
Bit by bit,
day by day.

TRUTH OR DARE

The Good Old Days

"Just wait until you are grown, you are going to wish that you were a child again," my mother used to tell me when I was girl. Then she would go on and on about the good old days. You know how she had to walk five miles to school in ten feet of snow, that they sometimes had to chop wood for the stove at the school and again for home. That they didn't have electric light so they had to do their homework using a kerosene lamp, and wore clothes made from flour sacks, blah, blah, blah. I remember thinking, boy if those was the good old days, thank goodness they are gone.

The Depression was on and times were hard, so people were forced to make do with what they had. While my parents were not rich by any means, neither were they poor. Both of them held government jobs. We always had food to eat and clothes on our backs. But growing up during these hard times made people practical. Nothing was thrown away or wasted. My mother even reused aluminum foil, wiping it off after it was used if it was still in good shape. My father, who people considered a snazzy dresser, kept the soles and heels of his shoes fixed and highly polished, instead of buying new ones.

According to some type of government survey I heard about recently, they say that those of us who were born in the 50's, 60's

CAROL GEE

and even the 70' s shouldn't even be alive today. It went on to say that, in the good old days we did not have childproof lids on medicines. But I had a mother who warned my sister and me at an early age that medicine was not candy. "You go ahead and poison yourself if you want too," mother said, "and I'll kill you."

It said we rode in cars without seatbelts or airbags. We had no childproof latches on doors or wall sockets. We rode bicycles without helmets, and sometimes even without brakes. I remember many times stopping my bike by dragging my tennis shoes on the ground. Now that I think of it, no wonder my mother had to keep replacing them. We licked batter from cake pans and nibbled on raw cookie dough. We climbed trees and fell out of them. We skinned our knees, cut ourselves, and sometimes knocked out teeth. My mother once told me that the tooth fairy didn't give out money unless the tooth fell out naturally. Teeth knocked out roughhousing didn't count. I think that she made that up.

The good old days were much simpler times. We children played hard trying to squeeze every inch of daylight of each day. We ate penny candy until we got a stomachache. Mary Jane's, Squirrel Nuts, Now and Laters, while Sugar Daddies, (the candy and not old men) were all-day suckers.

We licked H&S green stamps to fill up books to buy household items like waffle irons and other small appliances. And you received a toaster when you opened a bank account. Washing powder often came with a drinking glass or a dishtowel, and my mother bought the same brand until we had a whole set of glasses or cups or towels. Correcting a mistake in our little world was as simple as calling "do over"; major decisions were made by going "eeny-meeny miney mo." We got high on life, or inadvertently by handling mimeograph paper, or by spinning around until we got dizzy, instead of drugs and alcohol.

Where we almost never locked our doors, today new homes come

142

standard with security systems. Sitting outside talking to neighbors has been replaced by video games, watching television, or searching the web. Our nation's tall buildings obliterate the natural brilliance of fireflies.

Some say the good old days produced some of the finest risk-takers, thinkers, problem solvers and inventors. We tried things, sometimes failed, but tried again. Children had parameters and chores. We earned age-appropriate activities and privileges. The older we became the more privileges we were awarded. We messed up and we were punished. We survived.

Still I wonder what today's youth will remember when they speak about the good old days. And they will. When they do, will they remember a nation reved up on Starbucks coffee to keep them going; of road rage, gangster rap, and the rudeness of people on cell phones, whose inane conversation can be overheard in places normally reserved for silent reflection? Will they remember a country whose baby-faced soldiers are dying off one by one in countries with names that most Americans can't even pronounce, but seemingly always end in 'stan'?

Still, I'm not sure that I would have done anything differently growing up. Maybe had I known back then what I know today, perhaps I would have listened more when my mother spoke. Then I would have realized what she was trying to tell me. Things like being an adult is sometimes hard, or that two wrongs never make a right no matter how long you argue. And maybe I would have known a lot sooner what she knew even back then: that when my husband says I look 'fine' when I ask him how something that I am wearing looks, it means that I *really* need to change.

False Things

I was born without the faux (false) gene. Meaning that I don't do well with things that I wasn't born with. I have never had luck with wigs, fake fingernails or any of those kinds of things. Sure I have tried them. I was in the Air Force when I discovered mascara, eyelash curlers, and the like. Before that, my only experience with eye makeup was when I used my mother's eyebrow pencil (the one that she had worn down to a nub and tossed in the trash) to line my eyes in the eighth grade. Everything was fine until I forgot to wash it off before I came home. Suffice it to say that when she saw it, I learned that 'raccoon eyes' was not a term of endearment. Barely having time to use the restroom we were so busy cleaning it with a toothbrush, after Basic Training my sister soldiers and I finally were able to go all out with makeup and fixing ourselves up.

It turns out however that I was allergic to certain brands of mascara. I learned this the hard way when my eyelids puffed up and some of my lashes came out in the middle. I poked myself in the eye every time I tried to curl my eyelashes with an eyelash curler. Who thought of all these contraptions anyway? But you see I was away from home for the first time and I wanted to try everything.

Then someone suggested that my eyes would look nice if I wore false eyelashes. My dorm mate demonstrated step by step how to apply them. I tried to follow her lead. I combed them out like she showed me, ran a thin line of glue on the end and pressed them to my eyelid. Then I let them set for a few minutes before I lined them with an eyeliner pencil to make them look more 'natural.' I got make-up in my eye. The final steps were applying several coats of Mascara then giving it a turn with the eyelash curler. Then I would supposedly have that 'come hither' look that would beckon cute guys to me. I poked myself in the eye. Then my eyes started to water. I had to wait until they stopped so that I could see to complete my make-up.

I decided to wear them to a party that night. My 'come hither' look must have worked because a cute guy asked me to dance. He and I, along with James Brown, were busy "Making it Funky" when suddenly my vision became cloudy. It was like looking through a veil. I thought that it was because I was not wearing my glasses, which I needed to be wearing. But that would have ruined my 'look.' However, to my dismay I discovered that one of my false eyelashes had come off and was now resting on my lower eyelid next to my cheek. In the middle of the dance I ran to the restroom. I took off the one remaining eyelash and threw them both into the toilet and flushed twice.

False fingernails came next, but one by one they, too, embarrassed me. One time popping off and sailing somewhere across the room. Another time one came off and landed in my date's lap. But he was a gentleman. He plucked it off his lap and gave it back to me with a smile and continued eating his dinner.

Not satisfied with my hair, I tried wigs. Back then the Cleopatra look with its long fall and full bangs was in. I chose an auburn colored one, a shade richer than my own sandy hair at the time. A Big Afro followed. After all, it was the seventies, the age of Jimmy Hendricks, and "Power to the People" and all that. But because my own hair was long and soft, I had to tease it and spray it with so much hair spray that it triggered a severe coughing spell each time I did. Outside an Idaho wind complete with sandstorm attacked. Like right out of one of those westerns the wind whipped up out of nowhere and all of sudden, my 'fro' was all dusty (remember all the hair spray) and was now leaning to the side. I remember thinking that the only thing missing was John Wayne saying "Hold on to your hair there, Pilgrim."

Through the years I have tried other things. Acrylic nails were wonderful. I wore them for a while and they made my own nails draw beautifully underneath and looked quite natural. But when I finally took them off my own nails were so soft they even hurt. Then I tried on press-on nail to see if I liked them. A co-worker let me try one of hers when I admired the ones that she was wearing. They were painted a light pink tint that complimented my hands.

Wearing one on my little finger, I turned my hand right; I then turned it left. We women like to admire things from all angles. It looked really nice and I had just about decided that I would get some the next time I was at the drugstore. However later that evening I came home, washed my hands, and made dinner. It was while I was cleaning up the kitchen after dinner that I happened to glance down at my hand. The fingernail was gone. Then I spotted it in the dishcloth. Thank goodness. I was praying that it had not fallen in the dinner and my poor husband had not eaten it.

I wasn't through trying things, so not long ago, after a pedicure, I decided that what I needed to complete my look was a toe ring. I had seen a lady wearing one and I liked the way it looked. I noticed that the 99 Cents store carried them, and hey at 99 cents this was a bargain. So I bought one and put it on the second toe of my right foot. It sprang off and flew across the room. I tried again. It flew off again, this time one of the cats ran after it. It appears that it was too fat for my toe. I am wearing it as a ring now.

I am not a quitter, so back to the 99 Cents store I went. This time I bought a card with three different ones on it. Surely one of these would work. The smaller ones worked. Excited, I ran to show my husband how cute it looked. I think he was impressed when I stuck my foot near his face so that he could get a good look. He had this look on his face. I could tell he really liked it.

Perhaps all these experiences have just reinforced the notion that everything is not for everyone. This can sometimes be a hard lesson to learn and to come to terms with. Perhaps that is the reason that I have no tolerance for false friends. Or people who pretend to be something that they are not. For in me what you see is what you get, no more, no less.

Undershirts

While nearly all the girls in my fifth grade class wore bras as symbols of their impending womanhood, I wore an undershirt. Was this another one of my mother's attempts to keep me from being 'fly' I wondered? She declared it was not when I got up the nerve to ask. Still I was suspicious, after all, I still remembered the black and white saddle shoes, and her making me wear the gingham skirt complete with Rick-rack hem that I made in home economics, with knee-socks. The fact that I didn't have anything to put in a bra was incidental. At best my chest looked like two fried eggs with the yolk intact. Still ,I just wanted to belong.

I wore an undershirt from October to around the middle of May. Not even the sleeveless vest type with the v-neck would do. Only the round-neck, capped-sleeved ones would satisfy my mother. Granted the extra layer was welcomed as we walked five blocks to school in the cold and snow. For unlike my new home, Atlanta, where everything shuts down when 1 1/2 inches of snow touch down, Washington D.C. where I grew up didn't close schools until snow drifted up past our thighs.

During those winter months, I could explain away my undershirt by stating temperature statistics courtesy of the weatherman. But when the first week of May came and mother had not yet declared

my sister and me undershirt-free it took more creative explanations.
Had I thought of it without my undershirt there would have been
nothing between my chest and me since, unlike the other girls, I was
still without a bra. After a time though I declared myself undershirt
free by taking it off in the girls' restroom and tucking it into my book
bag, then putting it back on before leaving school for home. I simply
kept my back turned for modesty sake when changing into my gym
clothes

Yet I had no concept of cotton or its toil on mankind until I was
grown and went into the service. I had heard my mother speak of
ancestors who had labored in the fields. I remember the first I ever
saw it in its raw state. I was en route to Non-Commissioned Officer's
Leadership School in Phoenix, Arizona. An airman from the Base
Motor pool in Phoenix, Arizona had just picked me up from the
airport and we were riding along when I spied rows and rows, and
fields and fields of some crop.

Curious, I asked the young airman, who was Caucasian, what it
was. "It's cotton," he said, in a voice that implied since I was black
I should have recognized it. Sitting up straight in my sharp "Dress
Blues" with a chest full of ribbons and stripes that outranked him
thus demanded respect, I proclaimed in my most dignified voice that
the closest that I had *ever* gotten to cotton was from the items my
mother bought from the store.

As is happening more and more these days, I am recalling these
incidents and life lessons that have made me strong. Perhaps it only
happens as we get older and we wonder what lies ahead of us. For I
can see now that my mother did the things that she did to keep me
safe and warm as a child. The people who toiled in fields of crops
like cotton and tobacco did the same. They did it so that their children
would have the choices and the advantages that they never had.
Through the eyes of an adult I can see clearly now what I could not

see as a child. As a girl I saw wearing an undershirt as a barrier to my happiness, while my mother saw it as love.

Positively Aging

A year ago I started receiving this newsletter by e-mail called "Positive Aging." It's full of useful information for mature adults and seniors, things concerning investments and changes in health coverage and benefits. A lot of what it discussed I found to be interesting and (dare I say?) true. Still one question remained. How was I selected and how did they know to start sending it to me?

How did they know that I am not say, nineteen or even twenty-five? For while some of my co-workers surf the Internet constantly while at work (I won't call their names), I limit my surfing between the hours of nine to five to business. I reserve my orders for 'Blue' the medicated cream for all my aches and pains and creams that supposedly eradicate crow's feet for the privacy of my own home.

Had they somehow overheard my groaning out loud about that single hair that persists in growing under my chin, even after I yank it out with industrial strength tweezers? However, now it is trying to play hardball for I noticed just last week that has returned, but now it is gray. Has someone been noticing how carefully I laugh now to obliterate the laugh lines that appear to be multiplying and somehow contacted the editors?

Do they know that my knees sometimes creak like castanets when

I bend, or where I used to flaunt my waistline with belts the size of bracelets, that I now take comfort in elastic? Oh no, had someone still detected the aroma of Ben-Gay that I hoped that I had covered by a splash of Estee Lauder?

Mother said that there would be days like this. I had always known that she had eyes in the back of her head. Had she been able to see the future too? That does explain why she always seemed to know what I was going to do before I did it. "Don't *even* think about going out of this house looking like that." She would say before I even finished dressing.

Like many children I was blissfully unaware of things like losing our green space, computer crashes, and Anthrax. While my parents probably worried about our future, I was oblivious to the complexities of life. I never feared the danger of mosquito bites. For me 'cooties' was the worse disease that you could get and I wasn't even sure what that was. Back then we girls could actually sing that Madonna song, "Like a Virgin" with a clear conscience for many of us were.

Yet I have come to terms with getting older, and I think I wear it proudly. I find myself rebelling in small ways. I have started to take more risks. Yesterday I pulled the tag off of a pillow. Nothing bad happened.

Still, details have started to get fuzzy as aging eyes have started to blur at the fine print. Perhaps it's time for a stronger prescription. However, vanity wins out as I get bifocals without the lines. Is there anything positive about aging? I certainly hope so, as alas the journey has begun.

What A Girl is Waiting For

A while back as I checked my e-mail at work, finger paused on the delete button to zap back to cyberspace or wherever it is that all unsolicited e-mail comes from, I came across yet another new web site. Like most of the stuff that has of late multiplied across my computer screen like dust bunnies, I wondered what *this* one was about.

Curious, I clicked on it to little sayings that were supposed to brighten your day and lighten your load that they asked you to share with a friend. Not one of them volunteered to lighten my load by doing any of my work, I noticed. However the very last one, "What A Girl is waiting for" caught my attention.

An animated slide show portrayed a young Barbie-type woman in a short dress sitting on a park bench swinging her crossed legs while reading a book. I hated her on sight as she was doing both of the things that I long to do: first cross my legs, which I find is getting harder and harder to do daily, and second, read a good book without being interrupted. Each click of my mouse the animation continued downward, displaying a list of things that Barbie was supposedly waiting for:

Her Knight in shining armor.
Yeah like they really exist. I think.

A Man with money to burn.
Women say point him out, and stand back out of the way.

A man who is tall, dark and handsome.
Do women still dream about this?

A man with a big house.
In the background they showed a lovely brick mansion. But women today are not fooled for they know it's usually up to the woman to decorate this mansion without spending a lot of money. For while the man may have money to burn, most of it is spent on a big screen TV, beer, and a trunk load of remote controls and they are well on their way to couch-potato heaven.

A man with a fancy car.
This one showed a red Mustang in the background. Now if they want to 'keep it real' it would be maybe a Lexus, an Infinity or SUV.

A man who will love only her.
Here they showed a happy bride and groom looking adoringly at each other. We know that this was only for the camera for as soon as the flash fades, the groom will be shoving cake in the bride's face or vice-versa, and laughing. Maybe it's just me. But I see this as a sign of spousal abuse.

This dream where a knight in shining armor comes charging in on a white horse sounds romantic when you are a young girl. Too soon, grown women realize that once the man rides it in, it becomes *our* responsibility to take care of it, feed it and clean up after it.

Newspaper and magazine articles on relationships don't help by telling us that we are more likely to be hit by a truck than to find a mate after a certain age. But real women shake this off. We say that we hope that it is a furniture truck, we could use a new bedroom suite.

Still the final slide was more telling. For where Barbie was sitting on the bench with nothing to do, we now see a skeleton. The final caption in bold print says it all: SHE IS STILL WAITING. Sadder still in my opinion was the final instruction: send this to a friend.

Strong Women,
Women of Strength

Whenever life throws me a curve ball, as life is so often prone to do, or whenever I am retaining water causing my pantyhose to cut off circulation to my waist, I am reminded of women who have gone before me; women who suffered more serious afflictions than swollen ankles and bloating.

Recently having celebrated a few milestones in my life: a BIG, BIG birthday, thirty years of marriage to the same guy, and the publication of my first book, I suddenly realized that my journey into womanhood was borne on the shoulders of many women who came before. I was spawned from a woman who hummed along to gospel songs like "His Eye is on the Sparrow" on the small radio playing in the background, whipping up a meal fit for a princess with food scraps, imagination, and love.

I am the product of a woman born of ancestors who retrieved from the earth remedies for everything that ailed me, from colds to a broken heart, things like sassafras and other herbs guaranteed to either kill you, or cure you. The latter forcing me often to pray, "Please Lord, don't let it kill me." From her I learned to use my imagination, and whatever else was handy to do what needed to be done.

In my veins flows the blood of women with black history in their heads. Who told me stories about women like Madame C.J. Walker who turned dressing women's hair into a mega business, proving that women could be financially independent. My 'village' consisted of a slew of 'play' aunts and others who, while braiding my hair, sowed seeds of wisdom and decorum to last for a lifetime. Women who cried tears of joy as each of my birthdays came and went and I dodged the bullet of teenage pregnancy and sidestepped the drug bogeyman.

Inside me live women who, while not slaves to fashion, were trendsetters in their own right. Who walked tall in hats and hand-me-down dresses re-stitched by hand to fit because they didn't have a sewing machine, reinforcing a life-long message that clothes do not make the man/woman. That it is what's inside you and not FUBU or any other designer-labels that should be the thread binding the fabric of a person's life.

Modern Sojourners all, my role models were women who learned first-hand that being a woman wasn't easy. Some were women alone by choice, others by death or other happenstance. Some remained with men who saw them only as bandages for their own wounds. Too late, these women realized that what the elders proclaimed was true, 'that if you lie down with dogs, you sometimes get up with fleas,' or worse. But with one hand on the Bible and the other raised toward the heavens, they stayed and lay in the hard bed that they made.

While many of these souls are too numerous to remember, a couple I'll never forget. Like Mrs. Yarbourgh, my second grade teacher, whose heart was as warm as the Washington, D.C. winters were cold; who looked beyond my slanted, cursive letters and saw the person in me. From her I learned to appreciate my individuality.

Or Mrs. Hunter, the manager of a military service club, who took a young, girl soldier into her home to recover from pneumonia, showing her that angels really do exist. There she introduced me to a world of beauty beyond the tumbling tumbleweeds of Idaho. Where reverently touching her 'objects de art' from lands far away, I learned to respect the beauty of cultures other than my own.

As I reflect on my life's accomplishments, I am indebted to all of these women who individually and collectively nurtured me. Daily I surround myself with others of extraordinary character and strength. Like a sister struggling to raise a male child alone in a world where every day young, black males live in fear of those around them. For, sadly, not only will her lectures to him be about respecting women and himself, but how he should act when or if he is ever stopped by a policeman.

It is these women to whom I pay homage and say thanks. For even on days when I stumble and sometimes fall from the weight on my shoulders that is life, I get up and dust myself off and continue on. For I see their images in my mind's eye, these courageous women whose unselfishness make me the person that I am today, these brave women, beautiful women, strong women.

On Being Perfect

I am jealous of those women who seem so put together. They know who they are with their little scarves tied just so. Every strand of hair is in place, even their weaves, and stays that way all day. Their makeup is perfect, and they wear an air of supreme confidence. Perhaps they too struggle like me to keep this look together, although it certainly does not show.

While I have never been unduly feminine, I have always been described as prissy. As a young girl, I loved playing dress-up. While my younger sister was a major tomboy who rode her second hand bicycle like a bat-out-of-you-know-where and beat up on neighborhood boys, I tried on my mothers old dresses that were destined for the ragbag. I traced my lips with red candies like lipstick before popping them in my mouth.

Strings of pearls, a hat complete with veil and high heels rounded out my outfit. If my mother was not home and I was feeling particularly brave, I would reach up to the top shelf of her closet where she kept one of two fox flings, the kind with eyes and tails, that women wore draped over coats and suits. I put that on although those eyes gave me the creeps.

Today when I feel like dressing up an outfit, I may choose a scarf.

Although I don't care how many books I have read on how to wear a scarf, mine never looks like those pictured. Once I wore one to work and opened the middle drawer of my desk to get a pencil, only to close the drawer catching my scarf inside. Attempting to get up from my desk I almost strangled myself. Another time the scarf ended up in my soup at lunch.

And have you ever noticed that there is always someone who can't wait to tell you when you have made a fashion faux pas? "I don't think that I've ever seen a scarf worn that way," they say. Or, "Girl, I have a blouse just like that, only mine buttons in the back." Which, I suppose, explains those darts beneath my shoulder blades now that I think of it.

Still, when I was young, I tried to be perfect. This desire for perfection resulted from my mother scolding me for simply, being. "Come inside so that I can comb your hair," she'd call. "I don't want the neighbors to think that I let you girls run around looking wild and crazy. I am not raising any heathens." That is why my adored ponytail usually ended up in braids after only a few hours.

This perfection fantasy even wound its way into my marriage. I tried to be the perfect wife so that my spouse would feel that he made a great decision in marrying me. So when my husband told me that he adored homemade pound cakes, I set out with gusto to make one. After all, I had always heard that the way to a man's heart was through his stomach. Years later I learned that this was just another one of those old wives' tales. For, in truth, the way to a man's heart is a little farther down.

Betty Crocker I was not. To my amazement there were a trillion recipes for pound cake. One said to add a pinch or cream of tartar. What in the world was cream of tartar and how much is a pinch, I wondered. Not having any, I wondered what would happen if I just left it out and did. The result was a beautiful golden creation. However only in the oven. Reaching room temperature it deflated like a balloon. Mortified I put it out by the trash only later to discover the neighbor's cat sleeping on it.

After many tries however, I perfected the perfect pound cake, only to learn that sweet potato pie was now what my darling craved. Though with confidence born of trial and error I have discovered what works for me and what does not. With maturity comes the freedom to be who I am. Not perfect, just myself, just me.

Love and Marriage

Whenever someone ask me how long I have been married and I tell them 30 years, they look at me like I have two heads or something. Then they ask me what it's like to married to one person for that long. What is the secret of your success they ask and wait with bated breath for me to say something profound.

"Love and Marriage, love and marriage, goes together like a horse and carriage," or so goes the music from the comedy, "Married with Children." As Princess of Double Dutch rope, we often sung this tune as we jumped, our body swaying to the rhythm. While "Susie and Michael sitting in a tree, K-I-S-S-I-N-G, first comes love, then comes marriage, then comes Susie with the baby carriage," was another. No one ever questioned why the two of them were sitting in a tree in the first place. Nor questioned that love and marriage was not always in that order, or happened at all.

Of all the gifts that I received when we got married, three toasters, towels, glassware, money and other items that I have never used, not one person gave me a manual on what to expect after I got married. For I had no answers to what it meant be to a wife, only lots of questions.

Boy, I could have used one of the many 'dummy' books that are out today, like "Marriage for Dummies." Or "What Do I Do *Now* After I Have Tripped Over the Broom?" Or what to do when the broom has tripped me up, and I have landed hard on my backside on a floor that needs scrubbing? And my spouse just recently discovered that he was allergic to every cleaning product ever made. Mr. Clean causes him to break out in hives, while Pine Sol makes him sneeze.

Still most of us pattern our relationships and marriage from the ones we observed in our homes when we were growing up, or from television sitcoms. When you are young, marriage takes on the equivalent of mystery meat, until you have been together for some time. You are lucky if you figure it out before the so-called seven-year itch begins.

You see before there was "SURVIVOR" or the "The Real World" or any of those so-called reality shows on television, there were people like us living our own reality There was the stigma of a mother (his) thrice married and thrice divorced. There was a fatherless young man stewing in his own private hell of abandonment that were it not for the military he might have ended up wearing a different kind of uniform where every night the doors clanked shut behind him. Between us were the reality of too little money and orders to different locations, either temporarily or permanently every two to three years and a host of other issues.

There was a young woman who ran away from home and joined the military because she was not ready to go to college and could not have afforded it had she been ready. To be her own person, she felt, meant leaving behind those she loved or loved her so much that she felt smothered by their extremely high expectations for her. To save her own life, meant leaving the only one that she had ever known far behind. Complete opposites—where he was quiet, she was a chatterbox; where she longed for affection, he didn't seem to need it; where he was calm, she was the energizer bunny; who like so many women needed him to constantly prove his love for her.

Once, when we were stationed at a base in South Carolina, one of two bases where we would eventually reside, after an argument over something I can't even remember now, I decided to punish him and force him to prove that he loved me. Yeah, like I'm the only one who has ever done that!

We had been lucky enough to rent a private home on the beach. The family who owned the house wanted someone to take care of it while they were stationed at an Army Base in Georgia. After meeting us they thought that we would be perfect, and didn't charge us nearly as much as they could have. They even left some items in the house for us, which was great, since we were newly married and had only a little furniture. They also left some clothes in a closet in the spare bedroom, so it was there that I chose to hide. I thought if he thought that something had happened to me then he would be sorry that he had been mean to me.

Obviously, I didn't think it through. Hiding in the closet, I heard him on the telephone to some of our friends. When they indicated that they had no idea where I was, I heard him pacing back and forth. I wondered how long I would have to stay hidden as I was getting hungry and had to go to the restroom. Finally, after what seemed like hours, I heard the door slam as he left the house. I suspected that he would drive around and check out the Air Base.

My legs cramped up and my stomach growled. I crawled from my hiding place. Naturally he was so happy when he returned to find that I was okay, that he promised never to fight with me again and I promised never to scare him like that again. I wish that I could say that I never did anything to make him prove his love for me. I really wish that I could say that. But I can't. I am sure that I did other crazy things.

To prove that we are loved, women and men do stupid things. We try to make each other jealous by dressing provocatively, by flirting, or making stories about someone desiring us. We host temper tantrums, give them the silent treatment and do everything that we can to drive him crazy.

On the college campus where I work they offer a course called "I Will be Married in A Year" or something like this. This is not for college credit, but for those with a spare $100 and wishing to obtain their MRS. Degree this is perfect. The course, I'm told, is one hour and twenty minutes for three nights. It covers everything from what to wear when trying to make a love connection to how to act on a date. It suggests that you enlist friends to introduce you to eligible people, there are even workbooks and lesson plans that help to put you in the right frame of mind for being receptive to meeting someone eligible. For how many times have you heard someone say that they would like to meet someone and in the next breath they tell you what they will not do in order to meet them. You suggest that they might visit places where meeting a man is possible, like a museum, art gallery, etc. They say those kinds of places don't interest them. That they don't go in for all that fancy stuff. Others suggestions are met with the same response. They are not ready to meet anyone.

A well-known female comedian once remarked that men with pierced ears make the best husbands. After all, they have already experienced pain and bought jewelry. Still, since no manuals were available to me when I got married, much of what has worked me has been trial and error.

Through the years we have built a reservoir of trust in our relationship. I have learned not try to change him and to accept him as he is. While it is still a challenge, I try hard not to fill in the silences, but allow him the opportunity to think and to say what he wants to say. Truthfully though, sometimes it's like watching paint dry and I have to bite my tongue not to finish his thoughts.

"Blessings forever now, five, ten, fifteen, twenty, twenty-five, thirty years of love" sang a well known, 'ole school' musical group some thirty years ago. Thirty years, how time flies.

Our Slips,
Ourselves

I used to love wearing a crinoline slip when I was a girl. You know that slip that puffed out your Easter dresses? I remember bouncing when I walked making my dress move up and down. Although there was a slight drawback for when I sat down, the crinoline made my dress fly up in the air, causing me to scramble to hold it down so that people could not see everything I wore underneath.

Trying to decide on what type of slip to wear is like trying to decide on what type of man you would like to marry. Some women prefer slips that they can wear for any type of outfit. Others want a special one to wear with dresses that have splits. Another dividing line is fabric and cost. For the magic lies in the pocketbook of the beholder. Is it better to buy the 'el cheapo' from discount vendors or an expensive one from catalogs or high end department stores?

Most women feel that one's slip should not show below their outfit. Some insist on a trial dating period, meaning that you should try one on before purchasing. A woman could devote her entire life looking for the perfect slip or the perfect man.

Still, women could really use one that has 'Smart Logic' like in men's shavers or other items, where it automatically recharges batteries when the capability dips below 96 percent to keep power and performance in top form. How about a slip that adjusts automatically to the outfit that a woman is wearing? It would adjust to wherever the split is—whether it is on the side, the front or in the back. It would rise up or down automatically much like fashion hemlines.

Though come to think of it, I am not sure that I am ready for all of that action going on under my clothing. After all, I am already creating sparks when my thighs rub together in my pantyhose. Adding a battery where sparks already exist is just asking for problems in my opinion.

Stories of slip disasters abound. And every woman has some kind of story. If not, then she has never worn a slip, and that I can't even imagine. Women rejoice in the telling for sharing is much like therapy. A friend tells this story:

She said that she was exiting the parking deck at work. That day she was wearing a half-slip under her clothes. With her typical 'bag lady' self, she had a shoulder bag slung over her arm, and was carrying her briefcase that contained papers she needed for a meeting that morning. She was also brown-bagging her lunch having just paid this semester's night school tuition. As she crossed the parking lot to enter the building, she felt her slip sliding. Hands full, arms full, something had to give. It was not going to be her lunch she thought, as she needed her lunch and her slip was clean. Luckily her slip didn't fall down because this woman knew her priorities.

Another said that she was standing in line in the cafeteria where she worked when it happened. She said that she wearing a half-slip that had once belonged to her ex-mother-in-law and that this was the only thing that she had left of hers. I remember thinking that the mother-in-law must have been a terrific woman.

Suddenly she felt something 'give' and to her dismay she glanced down to notice her slip down by her ankles. She said that she simply stepped out of it and flung it over her arm and finished getting her lunch.

With all the modern technology that exists today, cell phones that you can hook up to your PC and computer keyboards that type by voice activation, you would think that someone would come up with a slip that fits every outfit that women own. Women spend too much time adjusting them and doing other things that really requires privacy and too much obsessive/compulsive behavior for most public events.

We fiddle with the straps adjusting them so tightly that is often difficult to sit and breathe at the same time. Using a large safety pin, we pin it up high around our waist. Or we roll up the waistband, which means that at any given time the front is usually much higher then the back. And using a safety pin could be dangerous if we are wearing one those H20 (water) bras.

My mother, were she alive today, would be so disappointed in me if she knew how many times I failed to wear a slip underneath my clothes. In truth, not wearing one makes me feel a little naughty. That she certainly wouldn't have liked. Still professionalism and modesty dictate that I wear them. So, to feel a little naughty, I will have to do something else. Wearing white shoes after Labor Day comes to mind.

Chocolate

I was walking back to my desk one afternoon when I felt it: this sudden euphoria, this incredible feeling from my first bite of the chocolate bar clutched tightly in my fist. You know how it slowly melts in your mouth, its creamy deliciousness on your tongue pulling you into a sort of ecstatic trance. For a moment I felt centered, as if the stars in the sky were all aligned. For a moment even the run in my pantyhose where the two legs are separated that is now large enough that a tractor-trailer could sail through it, or a desk cluttered with spreadsheets for the grant that I was working on were the farthest things from my mind.

No other flavor I know has the near mystical power of chocolate. From the nearest 'mom and pop' diner to the finest restaurant there is sure to be a confection sporting names like Death by Chocolate or Chocolate Overboard, where several layers of fudge cake is drenched with a chocolate sauce, smothered by chocolate frosting, topped with chocolate sprinkles, and lightly kissed with a few chocolate curls. Vanilla Overboard does nothing for us and does Death by Lemon even exist?

Even the movie industry has picked up the hype. Although I have long suspected that they were slowly running out of topics from which to make movies, judging from today's choices. There is a fairy tale-like movie out called "Chocolat" where this woman comes into a town, not with guns blazing, but with chocolate and turns the town around. Then there was another, "Like Water for Chocolate" I believe it was called. While "Willy Wonka and the Chocolate Factory" rounds out the kiddy fare.

Some time ago, I came across a cute little book, entitled "Hand Over the Chocolate and No One will Get Hurt." To me, that says it all, for chocolate, unlike some men, has been there for many a woman in times of crisis. At the first sign of PMS, women reach for a bag of Potato Chips with one hand and a Snickers bar with the other. Long for a kiss and your man isn't around? A Hershey one is a start. For truly, there are times when chocolate can solve a problem.

When I was child, all the 'aunts' in my support network always carried some kind of candy around in their purse. Usually it was peppermint that came in a variety of shapes. Mrs. Hemingway, one of mother's customers, once gave me this candy called Horehound candy. I believe it was really medicine and she mistook it for candy. The taste was to 'die for' literally, for as soon as I put it in my mouth, I thought I was going to die. It was light brown in color with taste sensation of sugar, licorice, and a mystery ingredient—tar I think. Was it just me or did you ever notice that old people never offered you any good candy?

Big on learning, my mother often took my sister and me on field trips. Once we visited an Amish community where everyone dressed in black and performed all their chores by hand. I think she wanted us to see that a person couldn't actually die from doing chores as my sister claimed. Still I was skeptical; after all, there was still that 'black clothes' thing.

Another time we went to Hershey Pennsylvania, the birthplace of chocolate. This was a chocolate lover's dream for there were tubs and tables and trays of chocolate everywhere the eye could see. In my mind's eye went an "I Love Lucy" episode as I watched chocolate slide off of conveyer belts almost too fast for the (mostly all women) employees to keep up with. But somehow they did. And I didn't see any of the women stuffing chocolates in their bra, for after all, this was a family outing.

Still the peace that comes from chocolate is short lived. I still worry about the state of world today, the economy, and what continually wearing elastic might be doing to my waist. However, I find peace wherever I can. Only yesterday I found it for a few brief moments. I ate a Snickers Bar.

What I Did on My Summer Vacation

Unlike Tony Bennett who left his heart in San Francisco and somehow lived to sing about it, my mother's heart always remained rooted to her native Virginia. And while Tony's song went on to become very popular, as did another, Sweet Home Alabama, I don't ever remember hearing a song written about Virginia.

In her early twenties, my mother left the family's farm for Washington DC where she used the money from dressing women's hair to supplement her salary as a Civil Servant. While some people went on vacation to the ocean or to the beach, for long as I can remember, the second week in August found us on a road trip bound for Virginia.

Hopping the Greyhound Bus with our fried chicken wrapped in waxed paper and sipping Grape Koolade, now watered down from the ice that kept it cool, we watched the world go by much like 8 millimeter reels of sights without sound. As always, the trip turned into an inner journey where, even as a child, I wrote the Great American Novel in my mind from the images that flashed before me.

We always stayed with my aunt, who eventually had 11 children, bringing to mind that nursery rhyme about the old woman who lived in a shoe, but provided lots of playmates for my sister and me to play tag, hide and seek and any other games that came to mind. With the innocence of youth, we sipped the nectar from the honeysuckle flowers that grew with abandon. And we kept one eye out for snakes as we picked blackberries for cobbler, staining our lips with their sweet/tart juice. Realizing early on that old saying, the blacker the berry the sweeter the juice, wasn't reserved only for berries.

Pennies in hand, we sneaked off to Cole's store for cookies or penny candy that actually cost a penny. Here we bought all the Squirrel Nuts and Mary Jane's that we could carry. At night Moon Pies replaced mints on our pillows, a bit crumbled by the babies, but still eaten by us kids.

To get to Mr. Cole's Store, we had to jump a creek and climb up a steep hill overgrown except for the natural path worn from years of travel by grown ups and kids alike. This was the same creek where we caught tadpoles before they turned into frogs. Never once imagining as a child how many frogs I would have to kiss as an adult before my own prince would come.

But while we were catching tadpoles and putting them in a jar, segregationists were voting to close the county's only public school down rather than to integrate it. And closed it down for five years, embroiling Virginia in what would later become part of the landmark Brown vs. Board of Education firestorm.

Yet Second Sunday found us in my mother's childhood church fanning ourselves with paper fans that advertised local funeral homes or pictured the Rev. Martin Luther King. These fans stirred the air around yet barely kept the sweat at bay. It was here that we prayed even for the hate-mongers and gave thanks to Him from whom all blessings flowed. We prayed for the repast for which we were about to receive. For set up under the trees were tables where platters of every food imaginable were arranged by women in dresses of every hue, rivaling some the world's finest gardens.

From summers past, we knew to get some of Ms. Mamie's sweet potato pie and Ms. Foster's fried chicken first, before it was all gone. And even as children we knew that Ms. Johnson's potato salad was food poisoning just waiting to happen.

Through it all I learned to appreciate the simple things in life—the love of family and getting in touch with one's roots. And while the summers of my youth have turned into the autumns of time, today if I close my eyes I can still conjure up the memories of my childhood summers in Virginia. Sometimes it's brought on by the smell of freshly mowed grass or the smell of chicken frying (other people's for mine is usually baked as I am watching my cholesterol). Sometimes it's a feeling; most likely a hot flash. Perhaps it's what mother and Tony Bennett had always known—that home is simply where the heart is.

The Forgotten Woman

Have you seen her? She is of average build, about five foot six, brown hair, blonde hair, red hair, only takes off about 10 pounds when questioned by an authority figure about her weight. Last seen she was carrying the whole world on her shoulders, stumbling a few times, still somehow managing to stay on her feet.

Someone said that they saw her at the grocery store, calculator in hand, juggling it and a fist full of coupons trying to stretch her meager dollars to feed her family. Someone else said that they thought they spotted her in the kitchen, with her *supermom* apron tied on tight to keep her business dress clean. They said that she was up at the crack of dawn making pancakes because she wanted her family to have more than cold Cornflakes and even colder milk before they headed out to work and to school.

Still another said that he saw her before she turned in for the night. She sorted through tall mounds of laundry, tossing a load of whites in the washer. Her saw her bend over as she picked up after Susie, picked up after Billie. He said she walked the dog, and fed the cat.

Does anybody recognize her? She strives to have dinner on the table right at 7:00PM every night even when her head is still hurting from bumping it on glass ceilings that appear to be daily getting lower and lower. And, with her "Stepford Wives" persona firmly in place, she runs to the kitchen for more milk for Billie, who spilled his first glass by elbowing his sister. Mopping up the spill with one hand she pours her husband more iced tea with the other. Susie wants catsup for her green beans. Gross as that is, at least she is eating her vegetables, so back into the kitchen she goes. While the family is enjoying their meal, hers is getting cold.

She is the one the relatives always call to patch up arguments, to referee verbal scrimmages among sisters and brothers. After all, she's the oldest, the calm one, the one least likely to poison them all in their sleep. She is the one they call when the light bill is due, or the phone company is threatening to cut off service, because the bill is over $300 and nobody knows who keeps calling them collect from Pennsylvania when they live Florida.

Are you her, this forgotten woman? Most likely you are. For this pattern of trying to be everything to everyone is learned at an early age. It was the way our mothers did things. Indentured servants to their family, they possessed an awesome ability to make everyone happy. After all, wasn't the joy on a husband or child's face its own reward?

Did they resent it we ask? Truthfully many never give it much thought. When they did, they said that it is just the way it was. Remember how many times your mother admonished you stop being so selfish? To never eat the last thing on a platter but wait to see if someone else wanted it? It didn't matter that you were still hungry and wanted it yourself. Did anyone ever question why mothers ate only the chicken backs and necks? No, they were *not* her favorite parts. She did it to ensure that everyone else had enough of the good pieces.

As women we must learn to take care of ourselves. I'm not saying to think only of yourself and let your family and others go wanting. I'm saying that we must realize that we can not be all things to all people all the time. We are not superwomen, which has been proven by the high rates of heart attack, stroke, and depression among women today. People don't usually die by us telling them no. No matter what your husband says.

I am reminded of a conversation that I had with a friend not long so who said that she was fed up always being the only one who helped out with any family responsibilities that she finally asked her sister why she never helped. She was surprised at her sister's reply because it was so simple. Her sister said it was because she never asked her for help.

There is no shame in asking for help when you need it. And it's not selfish to lie down when you are not feeling well. The shame is in being the forgotten woman when you are much too important for your loved ones to forget.

The Difference between Men and Women

A while ago my husband and I were chatting about relationships when I just happened to pull out one of those psychological/ personality tests from a magazine and suggested that we take it together. You know where you rate your compatibility, or your personal happiness quotient. Mostly A's mean you are woman, hear you roar; mostly B's declare that you are okay, even if your weave has seen better days; mostly C's demand that you get thee to a therapist's couch quick.

I confess to a weakness for these, for they tend to validate what I already know about myself–that I am a totally awesome female. Naturally I aced the *Are you confident* test. He, on the other hand, approached this with as much enthusiasm as he did a root canal. But did it anyway probably hoping with any luck, this torture would soon end and he could get back to his football game. Fortunately he scored in the mostly B's category. Feeling somewhat cocky, (no pun intended) he then began a treatise on the differences between men and women.

Snips and snails and puppy dog tails. Why, this sums it up in a nutshell. Compared to 'sugar and spice and everything nice' the sexes don't stand a chance. So, really into this, my husband expounded on these differences. Here is his take on them:

Men can go to the restroom without a support group. I say that men are just leery about things that they don't understand.

Men don't mooch off other people's plates. What do men have against sharing? Is it our fault that for some odd reason what they are eating always seems to look better than ours? And he has to admit that there is something kind of intimate about eating food off your loved one's plate. After all, we would never do that to a stranger.

My husband has this habit of giving me his vegetables when he is getting full when we are dining out. "Here honey, you want some of these green beans, or some corn? I am getting full." He says. I notice however that he never offers me any of his steak, prime rib or shrimp.

Men never have strap problems in public. And women never have problems with their fly. Nor do we feel the need to constantly look down to see if the lower part of our anatomy is still there. Believe me you would probably *know* if it were not.

A man only needs one wallet, one pair of shoes in one color, and he is ready for all seasons: So tell me again, why is it that we always ask him to help us decide which one of our ten pairs of Taupe colored shoes goes better with the new dress we just bought?

Men can be trusted not to trap you with "so do you notice anything different?" Okay so we woman can sometimes be rather superficial. But after having Tae-boed ourselves silly, lost 10 pounds, and dyed our hair, we want somebody (meaning men) to notice it. And no, it does not count if we have to point out these changes.

Men know stuff about tanks and other heavy equipment: I admit there are days that I wish I had a tank. These are the days when I am driving beside some maniac chatting on his cell phone and drinking coffee while driving 50 miles an hour in a school zone and inching closer and closer into my lane.

Men say that they don't understand women. Why do we do the things that we do? Why do we have to have so many pairs of shoes? Women wonder why men can not ask for directions when driving instead of driving *us* around the bend? Perhaps this sounds familiar:

Woman: "Honey why don't we stop somewhere and ask for directions. The invitation says that dinner will began promptly at 7:00, and it is now 6:50."

"Who's driving here, me or you?" (Women think, but don't say it, "if I was driving we would sitting down to eat by now")

"Can we please stop at a gas station or something?" she asks.

"Why? Do you have to go to the restroom? Can't you hold it for another minute because we are almost at our destination?" he says.

Woman (almost in tears, and it is *not* because she has to go to the restroom) "The sign now indicates that they are headed back toward the freeway."

"I know where I am going, so stop bugging me. I *got* this." He says.

Perhaps some of these other scenarios may sound familiar:

One Saturday morning dawned warm and sunny so my husband decided that he would wash both of the cars. I am in the kitchen making coffee.

(Him) "Honey, I think that I am going to wash the cars. Where is that bucket I always use?"

"It's where it usually is, in the laundry room." He goes into the laundry room and finds bucket. He comes back into the kitchen.

"Where is that little brush that I use to scrub the tires?"

"Is it not in the bucket?" We women do have to ask this, trust me, for often things are right there in front of men's faces and they can't see them.

"No," he says like he thinks that I'm an idiot, or that I think that he is.

I think for a minute, then look underneath the kitchen sink where I suspect I left it when I last scrubbed the kitchen floor. He would not know anything about that. I hand him the brush.

"Where are those old cleaning towels that I always use?"

My patience is now wearing thin, but I try not to let it show. I promised myself that I would not nag, nag, nag like my mother used to.

"Do you live here? Do you live in this house? Don't you know where anything is?" I ask. I go into the pantry where they are folded neatly on a shelf and throw a bunch at him.

He smiles that little smile that he knows I love but am not feeling right now, as if to say, "Got You." Forget coffee, I think, I need something stronger.

After finishing with the cars, he decides that he is hungry. I volunteered to make him some breakfast when I made mine, but he wanted to do the cars first. He opens the refrigerator door and leans in to peek. Really getting into the research, he leans heavily on the refrigerator door.

There are all sorts of things in there. Fixings for a sandwich, leftover spaghetti, cold chicken. There is leftover Chinese food from the night before. Granted once he heats it up and eats it he will be hungry again in an hour. Nothing seems to catch his fancy. He goes back upstairs to the sitting room. He turns up the television; loud. The next time he has a physical I'm recommending that he have his hearing checked. I suspect that he is going deaf by the way the volume continues to rise. I know that I am.

Half an hour later he comes back down to the kitchen. By now, looking in the refrigerator has become a spectator sport as he again leans heavily on the door. I can see this from the family room couch where I am now folding laundry. He sighs, loudly. Both cats wake up from their nap and go to investigate.

"Are you hungry?" I ask. "It will be a while before I cook, but there is spaghetti and chicken and stuff in there. Take a look in some of those containers. Take the lid off, you can't see anything with the lid on."

I am on a roll now. " Stuff is not going to reach out and grab you. And hurry up, you are letting all the cold air out of the refrigerator. And please stop leaning so heavily on the door, we paid a lot for that. Leaning on it like that can't be good for it." It's finally happened. I have become my mother.

He opens up a container and goes to the microwave. I smell spaghetti. He looks at me and smiles. Having finally run out of steam, I am gritting my teeth. I think that I need a day at the spa, or a drink, maybe both.

Still these things are small compared to the grand scheme of living and loving. As husbands go, he is pretty special. I have realized that I may never understand the things my husband or any man does.

Once, in exasperation, I asked him why he did some of the things he did sometimes. To my surprise he looked at me and, with a smile, replied, "I don't know."

I know it's silly. But somehow I am comforted by the knowledge that while I don't know why he does the things that he does, neither does he. Perhaps men and women are not so different after all.

A Love Relationship Built on Stuckey's

Some of my fondest memories of the twenty years that my husband and I spent in the Air Force were when we received a change in military assignment stateside and we had to drive to our destination. Never much of long distance driver, although I have been forced to do it a time or two, I usually rode shotgun with the map while he did the driving. I am not really certain which was worse, my actually driving or map reading.

Leaving early in the morning before there were many cars on the road, we would drive until dusk. Cloaked in the warm cocoon of our automobile, it sometimes seemed that we were the only two people in the big wide world as the dawn lit up the morning sky. The only stops we made were to fill up our gas tank, take a restroom break, and get something to eat.

As we drove along the highways guided by billboard after billboard of the yellow and red signs for Stuckey's we wondered what adventure lay ahead for us at the new duty station. Twenty-two miles to Stuckey's. How long would it take before we got military quarters? Fifteen miles to Stuckey's and Pecan Heaven. Would we like the new base? Turn left one mile and you are at Stuckey's. What would the people be like? Would they be friendly?

While my husband pumped gas at the Texaco station that always seemed attached to the store, I went inside. First a quick trip to the restroom, then visit the rows and rows of gift ideas. Plates with the name of whatever state we happened to be in, or a bird, or state flower figurine. Perhaps this is where my husband's aunt, who raised him, got all the plates that hung on the walls of her dining room in the row house where she lived in Baltimore. I bought one that I hoped she did not have. Cow salt and pepper shakers and toothpick holders– exactly what I need for my new kitchen, I think. I buy a pecan roll, which I pulled apart to savor the richness as we sped along the highway.

Our car eating up the miles, we cruised on, sometimes talking about our hopes and dreams for the future. Other times we were quiet, each of us wrapped in our own thoughts. As soon I get settled I need to start studying for the sergeant's exam that will get me promoted to the next grade. Both of us could use some new uniforms and I need to get some steel-toed combat boots. We are both getting hungry so he asked me if I wanted to stop at the next Stuckey's up ahead. He smiled that smile that I have grown to love, his beautiful eyes hidden by his military-issue sunshades for he already knew the answer.

While we were not in a hurry, our trips took longer than normal because of our many stops. At each stop I bought some trinket to help me remember places that we passed along the way with Stuckey's as our beacon of familiarity in otherwise unknown country.

Recently I read somewhere that like so many icons, the Stuckey's with the red and yellow billboards have nearly all but disappeared and are gradually being replaced by something called "Stuckey's Express". I should not be surprised as we live in a world of 'express' this and 'express' that, stop, now go, and hurry up and wait.

Still, the old Stuckey's will always hold a special place in my heart. Not for the pecan rolls and whatnots alone, but because it made me realize that what I mistook for an emotionally distant man who kept his feelings bottled up inside, was in actuality a man sometimes unable to put into words what he was feeling. But showed that he cared about what made me happy, even if that meant stopping at every Stuckey's that he saw, thus showing me the window to his soul, proof positive that action does speak louder than words. And if we look closely, we can sometimes see them with our hearts.